SHARPEN THE BLADE

THE V V INN, BOOK SIX

C.J. ELLISSON

Red Hot Publishing
P.O. BOX 651193, STERLING VA, 20165-1193

First Print Edition May 2017
Print ISBN: 978-1-938601-39-2
Copyright 2017 C.J. Ellisson
All Rights Reserved

PUBLISHER'S NOTE

This is a work of fiction. Names, characters, places, and incidents are either the products of the author's imagination or are used fictitiously, and any resemblance to actual persons, living or dead (or undead ;-), business establishments, events, or locales is entirely coincidental.

For my adopted nephew, Pat Larson. May you continue to enjoy adventures with Eric—whether in dreams, through retold escapades, or via the pages of a book.

PREFACE

This book started as an extended epilogue. Meant as a gift to my newsletter subscribers, *Sharpen the Blade* was intended to fill in what occurs with our characters before they face their final *V V Inn* adventure in *Blood Reckoning*.

All of that sounds fine and dandy until the author starts writing with no direction and no clear idea of what she's doing. Plain and simple, my life fell apart after releasing book five in the series, *Blood Legacy*.

When I was sick, life had a very narrow focus: family, health, and work. I struggled daily to maintain a balance. If I focused on one, the others would suffer. Pretty soon, it became painfully obvious if I didn't focus more on my health, there would be no more books and no more time spent with family.

Right as I began to get a solid handle on my health and seemed to finally be past the worst life had thrown at me, my mother had a severe hemorrhagic stroke. At the time, I was hopeful for a close-to-full recovery. But after a while, my mother settled into her current fate and refused additional therapies.

About the same time, my father announced he was "checking out" as soon as my mom was healthier, that he'd had enough of life and was ready for it to end.

Nothing I said to either of them mattered. Nothing I did made a difference, and I slowly began to lose myself in the grief and heartache of losing two parents who were still technically alive. For the health of myself and my immediate family, I needed to pull back and allow my parents to live however they decided.

Therapy helped immensely and after a time I went back to work. But the words don't start flowing simply because you've decided it's time they do. My current manuscript was a rambling mess. It took me months to figure out the problem (after numerous re-plotting attempts), and then even longer to muster the desire to fix the issues.

How does one fix ten rotating points of view (POVs)? How do you make what was essentially an extended epilogue into a real book? You cut POVs and devise a real plot. Easier said than done.

It took a lot of work. Embarrassingly more work than any project I've ever done to date. I learned a lot about creating, about my processes, and about myself. Not all of it good, but all of it helpful.

It is my sincerest wish you enjoy this story. I can't say I didn't try with this one, because I sure as hell did.

As always, thank you for your support and interest!

Happy reading,

~C.J.

CHAPTER ONE: VIVIAN

I slip on the hooded trench coat and make my way toward the plane's exit. Despite the danger looming over us, I'm glad to be home. The return trip from Buenos Aires was long, tiring, and filled with conflicting energies. Rafe, my human husband, could hardly sit still, and Jon, my werewolf servant and our right-hand man, vacillated from texting furiously on his phone to pacing the tight confines of the cabin.

The air in the plane seemed to vibrate with tension from the three of us—and our stress dueled awkwardly with the excited optimism from our newest employee, Justin, a magic-using wizard and a former security consultant to the Tribunal of Ancients. We hired him to install magical safety wards around the resort, similar to what he did for the ancients, in addition to having him teach my husband how to use magic—an idea I'm still not thrilled with.

All these steps and more are necessary, I've been assured, in the grand scheme of surviving the upcoming dangers. Rafe, Jon, and I aren't looking forward to what's on the horizon—

hunting down the vampires I turned who have manipulator traits—but we know it has to be done. It's the only option we have to stand against Rolando and Persephone in their quest to transform the South American city into a present-day version of the ancient, and extinct, vampire-ruled Atlantis.

"*Liebling*," my husband calls before I descend to the tarmac of our Alaskan resort's private airstrip. "Your hood."

I nod absently and draw the lined fabric over my head. We've landed after nine at night, and while there's plenty of light this time of day above the Arctic Circle in early July, I know I'm in no real danger of catching flame or burning my sensitive vampire skin. Living half a millennia as an undead does have its advantages. It would take prolonged exposure at high noon for me to be truly worried about my safety.

"Come on, come on," Jon grumbles, every muscle in his body straining. "Let's get off this flying tube of death already."

I smile to myself and purposefully take the short staircase one step at a time, slowing down to irritate the powerful werewolf. "Are you anxious to see someone, Jon?" I say while looking over my shoulder at the man. His broad chest, straining the buttons of his customary flannel, tapers to a flat waistline. Which draws the eye down to his muscular legs hugged by faded jeans. Short brown hair is styled back, off his forehead, exposing his rugged good looks, and his hazel-green eyes appear to be searching the distance for something, or someone —an eagerness almost burning in their depths.

"What?" he stops, his expression freezing. "No, nothing like that." A quirky grin spreads across his face. "I need to use the bathroom, that's all."

My high heels meet the ground and I immediately step to the side, allowing him to rush past me. "Uh-huh. Sure." I know he started seeing someone last month, but for whatever reason, he's decided to hold back from sharing the details with Rafe and me. Maybe this one is becoming serious and he wants to make sure before telling us.

Rafe's mental voice reaches out to me through our mate-bond connection. *Or maybe he's afraid of how you'll react.*

Nonsense, I respond telepathically. *I've given him no reason to think I'd handle it poorly if he were to start dating someone.*

Rafe mentally projects a shared memory to me, one of me ripping the head off Vikram, a vacationing vampire, when he dared to feast upon my werewolf servant. Not one of my finer moments, as far as leaping first and looking later, but Jon is my responsibility and I had to act quickly or the fang head would have drained him. In Vikram's defense, he'd had a new addiction to werewolf blood to contend with and I could have handled the situation a little better.

You think? My husband interjects into my thoughts.

A frown mars my face as I watch Jon stride swiftly toward the airplane hangar. *It was extenuating circumstances. And Vikram wasn't trying to 'date' Jon, but suck him down like a supernatural juice box.*

Still doesn't mean Jon would feel comfortable telling us. Rafe stops next to me, draping an arm across my shoulders. "Let's go in." He glances up at the sky. "God, I've missed this place in the summer. The abundance of light feels intoxicating."

"It's greener than I expected," Justin says, joining us on the tarmac. "And more flat." His tall, lean frame is draped all in black, from his button-down shirt, an undershirt peeking out of the neck, to pants, heavy boots, and light jacket. Some of the fabrics appear faded and frayed at the edges, but the monochromatic color scheme affect is still the same. A hawkish nose and dark blue eyes dominate his facial features with dark, longish hair falling over his brow.

I smile and gesture past the spindly trees lining the runway. "We've got our share of hills and mountains, don't you worry. The resort property straddles tundra, a ski-worthy mountain, and denser forest near the national park border, too."

"Yeah, I noticed the terrain when we circled to land. I saw a lake and several streams from above. How's the fishing?"

Having never fished up here, I'm at a complete loss on how to respond. I look to my capable husband with a raised eyebrow.

"Most of our employees take advantage of all the area has to offer as far as hunting and outdoor sports," Rafe answers. "They'll be the best ones to let you know if there's any good fishing. But—most of them aren't on the property during the summer off-season. Maybe someone in the apartments can help you—or maybe Miranda, our human resources person. You'll meet her soon."

Justin nods and meanders after Jon, his head moving from side to side as he takes everything in. "Peaceful and quiet. I think I'm going to like it here."

Rafe lowers his voice and leans in to speak after the younger man walks away. "How do you want to handle the introduction of him to Asa and Eric?"

I squint in the bright light and shade my eyes. "I'm not sure. Is there ever a right way to spring a surprise like that on someone? But I do think we should tell the boys before they run into him unexpectedly."

"What if we're wrong and they aren't related?"

"True, that very well could be the case. And I admit, I don't see much of a family resemblance between the three, but the coincidence with the last name is too great. I know I recall hearing Asa say his parents divorced and his mother left the country with their older brother. How common is the surname Monson? It's got to be him."

"We'll just have to see, won't we?"

We walk together to the corrugated steel building, the scent of fresh forest growth heavy in the air. "Too bad we won't be here long," I say, my gaze touching on the greenery of the resort in the summer. "It's so pretty with all the flowers in bloom."

"Yeah, that pesky manipulator-vampire problem we have to deal with," my husband says with a sideways grin that quickly slides off his face and turns into a grimace. "When do you want to be back on the road?"

"In a few days, a week tops, if we can swing it. Really depends on how long it takes to find the information we need."

"How many journals did you fill?"

"I can't recall. Maybe fifty."

"Fifty? Geez. I might read fast, but not *that* fast," he says as we step into the shade of the hangar. "We need to find a way to quickly comb through the data contained in the pages."

"We've already talked about this—I'm not open to the idea of letting more people read my personal history contained within those pages. The knowledge could be dangerous."

"No, I figured you wouldn't be. How about we talk to Asa

and see about scanning the pages into a computer? Then we could search the contents easier."

Before I can answer, Jon's raised voice booms from the hangar and a moment later a sleek, muscular, reddish dog bounds from the building and rushes toward us, tail wagging, head down, and ears pinned back in a show of excited submission. The wiggling mass of happiness pauses at our feet and looks up at me with golden-hued eyes.

Jon races back out and skids to a stop when he sees us with the dog. "Oh, hey guys. Sorry about that." He pats his leg. "Come here, girl."

The dog doesn't listen, but continues to watch us while wagging her tail.

"She's pretty," Rafe says, bending to offer his hand to pet her. "Is she a red-nosed Pit Bull?"

Jon looks panicked for a second before quickly recovering. "Uh, yeah. I think so." He gazes down at the animal with a shrewd, and angry, eye. "That sounds about right."

I wonder what's eating him. He doesn't normally flounder on naming a dog breed. It's like the man studied them as a child or something.

"Where'd she come from?" Rafe accepts a kiss on the chin from the eager dog. "Don't you normally only have husky-wolf hybrids?"

Jon's face becomes expressionless as he answers. "I think Asa told me he adopted her from a shelter on his last trip to Fairbanks."

I study the animal and her gaze slides away. She quickly drops to her back and exposes her belly for a rub. A smile spreads across my face as I crouch to comply. My hand skims over her soft stomach as I note the distinct white blotch of fur under her neck. It looks like a moth or butterfly with spread wings. "She's a sweet thing. I like the marking on her chest."

A sigh escapes me. I forgot how much I loved having our own dog. No matter how much Rafe likes to tease and call Jon a furball, a werewolf isn't a dog, and a grown man isn't a damn pet.

It's not like I can invite Jon's hybrid animals into our bed for a cuddle on a cold night even if I wanted to. He confines them in the heated kennels after dark. And when I do see a dog on the property, most of them give me a wide berth. From past experience, I've found if a dog isn't around vamps much, our scent warns them away.

My wistful gaze travels over the fine-looking animal. "Guess that means she's staying with Asa in the basement, huh?"

"Uh... that makes sense," Jon says, his stare fixed on the dog. "Yes, she's probably staying with him in his suite."

"Do you know how old she is?" Rafe asks, a smile across his handsome face. He always did love having a dog in the house, too, and we used to have a Staffie, a smaller cousin to the Pit, years ago. "I take it she's housebroken?"

Jon shifts his weight from side to side. "No idea on the first question, and yes to being housebroken."

Stifling my personal desire to pick her up and bring her home with me, I rise and continue into the hangar past the Pit Bull, who quickly rolls to her feet to follow. "I'm not opposed to Asa having a pet in the main building, but if she starts destroying stuff he's going to have to move to a cabin."

A compact man with tan skin and dark hair emerges from the shade of the building. "Good evening, ma'am," he says, a smile splitting his face. "How was your flight?"

The man is Diego, our head pilot, mechanic, and all around fix-it-guy when it comes to anything aviation. During our trip south, we requested he stay in the States for emergencies, just in case there was a need from the employees left here.

"It was good, Diego," I say while offering my hand in greeting. He enfolds my hand in his for a brief shake. "Thanks for asking. Glad to be home."

"I bet. I'm through here for the night, just wanted to see if there was anything you needed before heading home."

A smile creases my face as the dog leans against my side and I reply, "I think we're good to go, thank you. I'll reach out to you in the morning if there's anything else. Thank you for waiting to see that we arrived safely."

"No problem. I'll have one of the maintenance crew deliver your luggage within the hour." He nods to Rafe, shakes his hand as well, and turns back to the way he came, heading toward the airport's office.

Jon calls the dog again with another generic command of *come here, girl*, but she stares off into the distance like she didn't hear him. She doesn't seem very obedient, or maybe she doesn't like Jon. I'm sure that will rub him wrong, as he's a bit of a self-proclaimed dog-whisperer when it comes to canines.

"What's her name?" I ask.

The werewolf's voice sounds low and gruff when he responds. *"Diablesa."*

"She-devil?" Rafe asks. "Isn't that a bit... harsh?"

"Quite fitting," the annoyed Were replies, "because the little bitch isn't listening right now."

A laugh bubbles out of me as I watch our groundskeeper try to control his anger over a dog that doesn't immediately jump to follow his every command. "If Asa's still experimenting with names, maybe he should try *Miraposa*, to match the butterfly mark on her chest."

The dog barks at my side, her tongue lolling out as she glances up at me, looking like she has a huge grin splitting her doggie face. I'm sure the large, open jaws help to reinforce the impression that she's smiling.

Rafe chuckles as he catches up to me. "Would you look at that. I think she likes the new name."

"Whatever," Jon says, stooping to remove a pile of fabric from the middle of the hangar floor. "She's his problem," he grits out with a sharp glare at the animal. "Not mine."

We travel toward the exit in the rear, and join Justin waiting behind the building, then proceed toward the SUV parked nearby. Rafe pauses by the back of the vehicle, leaning down to pet the dog again while we wait for Jon to catch up. "I like her. Her fur almost matches your hair, Dria." My husband addresses me by my real name, whereas, over the years, our employees adopted the nickname Vivian for me, as a play on words to the hotel's name—The V V Inn.

Justin sees us near the backdoors and climbs into the passenger seat, correctly assuming Jon will be driving.

"Two redheaded bitches at the inn," I say with a smile as the angry werewolf reaches us. "The employees won't know what to think."

Jon chokes and coughs, as Rafe laughs and opens the back door for me. I slide inside and the dog leaps up to follow, staying in the deep footwell to snuggle up against my legs. I rest a hand on her wide head as Rafe climbs in to join me.

"She reminds me of Cleo," he says. "The red Staffie we had at the Paris V V Inn a long time ago."

The memory floods back to me with a warmth blossoming in my chest. "You're right! She does. We still have a picture of us with Cleo hanging in the office. This dog's a little longer and leaner, with lighter eyes and nose, not to mention taller—but you're right. It's the coloring. God, I loved that animal."

His palm slides over my thigh in a reassuring touch. "Don't get too attached. Remember, she's Asa's."

Jon opens the driver's side door, gets in, and slams it hard, anger radiating off him in waves.

"Are you okay, Jon?" My brow furrows in concern and the animal whines at my feet.

"Just peachy." He starts the vehicle and pulls away. After a moment, he takes a deep breath. Perhaps willing himself to calm down. "Don't mind me. Must be tired. And I know we've got a lot to do, so it must be getting to me."

I look at Rafe, who shrugs as if to say he has no clue what's eating the man either.

Rafe takes out his cell phone. "How about I get the ball rolling and organize a debriefing at midnight? That should give us a chance to unpack and settle in a little." Jon nods as my husband starts his text. "Take us to the apartments first."

I lean down and put my face closer to Mariposa's. Yes, I have mentally re-named someone else's dog. Calling her she-devil, in any language, doesn't fit with her nature. "Ignore that grumpy werewolf. He stinks. You stick with me and I'll look out for you." She licks my jaw, exhibiting a sweetness I don't expect. Unexpected moisture fills my eyes. We've lived up here with no personal pets for so long, I've forgotten what unconditional love from one can feel like. The sensation fills me, and her adoring stare reminds me of a hug.

We won't stay for long on this visit, but when we're back

for good, I may have to steal this dog for my own. Asa can always get a new one on his next trip to Fairbanks. He can't be too attached to her yet, right?

I'd love to report a feeling of guilt at my highhanded thoughts of taking someone's pet, but nope. There's none. Being in charge should have its advantages.

Come now, you want to steal his new pet, liebling? How about we get one of our own?

He couldn't have had her long. It wouldn't hurt to ask.

By "ask" do you mean "tell"? He squeezes my knee gently to show he's teasing, but I ignore him anyway.

Jon drives to the employee apartment building and we spend time showing Justin around and introducing him to Miranda. In a few minutes, Justin's assigned one of the larger units, probably bigger than his tiny house in Buenos Aires, and given the keys with a map of the resort. At Miranda's prompt before leaving, Rafe takes Justin's picture on his phone for the young wizard's employee file, and he arranges to meet with him tomorrow morning for the laying of the new security wards and their first magic lesson—a prospect that still has me on edge.

I trust the man I married. Even when I don't agree with all his decisions. Like the one to learn magic. But I also respect his need to do something to keep us safe and strong, so I'll keep my mouth shut. For now.

CHAPTER TWO: JON

I enter the conference room a few minutes before the scheduled debriefing, erratic energy pouring off me. Sure enough, I'm not alone. The bald vampire sits stoically in the dark, peaceful and quiet, like he's meditating or some such shit.

Uncaring, I slam on the lights and flop into the chair next to him. "Vivian thinks you got a dog."

"What?" Asa says, confusion crinkling his forehead. "Why would she think that?"

I push away from the table to stand, anger fueling my movements, making them jerky. "Goddamn Candy. That's what." Running both hands through my hair, I grasp it in my fists and tug hard. "You're not going to believe this," I say, releasing my hair and starting to pace. "Get this—she shifted to the form of a dog and was at the airstrip—ready to meet Vivian and Rafe the second they got off the plane."

"Yikes," he says with a grin. "Talk about your girlfriend truly being a bitch." The scowl I send his way wipes the smug smirk off his face. "Why in the hell would she think that was a good idea? And why haven't you told Vivian about her yet?"

"I have no clue why she did it. No fucking clue!" My pacing increases in speed. "And Jesus, Asa, I can't believe you're grilling me on the *why*. We're talking about the master vampire I've *pledged my life to*. Don't you think I should make sure things are solid between me and Candy *before* I introduce her to someone who can essentially crack her mind wide open?"

He smiles, not trying very hard to hide his amusement at my predicament. "Kind of like a teenager afraid to introduce his new, wild girlfriend to his conservative parents?"

A groan escapes me. "Fucking hell, man. That's right, make jokes. It's really helpful."

"All right, all right. Don't get your panties in bunch. Did you tell Candy you were coming back today? Maybe it was a case of being in the wrong place at the right time."

The energy inside pushes me to continue pacing. Or punch something. Pacing seems safer. "I texted her at our last refueling stop. I asked her to hang back at the cabin until I had a chance to introduce her properly."

"There you go again, sounding like you're bringing her home to meet your folks."

I whip around and shoot the fangy bastard another deadly glare. "Not helping, man."

He raises both shoulders. "Fine. I'll try to help. What do you expect me to do?"

"I need you to pretend you adopted a dog in Fairbanks and texted me about it. Oh, and you named her Diablesa."

"Dia-what?"

I sound it out, exaggerating the syllables. "Dee-a-bless-ah.

Means she-devil. It spilled out in anger when Viv asked the dog's name. But I think she's renaming her to Mariposa now."

"Renaming my dog? That's not cool, man."

"She's not your fucking dog!" I storm to the hall and lean my head out, checking to make sure we're not overheard. "What a freakin' nightmare. I don't know how the hell I'm going to handle this."

"The truth usually works pretty good."

"Thanks for the obvious, you bald bastard."

He smooths a hand over his freshly-shaven skull. "I'm not bald, man. I shave it."

With a rush, the frantic energy drains out of me and I collapse into the chair again. "Maybe Candy has a reason for doing what she did."

"Hey, that's a good point. Maybe she did. You should ask her."

Sounds from down the hall indicate Eric and Pat are about to join us.

"Don't say anything to them, okay?" I plead. "I need to talk to Candy first."

"Whatever, man. They'll know I didn't get a dog in Fairbanks."

"Shit!" I slam a fist into the table. "That means I have to tell them. And they'll blow it in front of Viv and Rafe. I know it."

"Give them some credit. They're not completely without merit."

The two young Weres pile in, pushing and shoving in their exuberance, like a bunch of rambunctious puppies.

"Dammit," I say, ignoring them while they act like idiots. "This is all I need on top of everything else." Another thought

I wanted to ask him bubbles up. "Please tell me you've noticed the stuff Rafe's been doing lately? I can't be the only one paying attention."

Before Asa has a chance to respond, Pat says, "What are you guys talking about? What are you worried Rafe will notice?"

I close my eyes for a moment. I need to calm the fuck down and handle this better. They're just young guys and don't deserve my scrambled, frustrated wrath.

Before I can decide what to say, Asa saves me. "Hey, guys, I'm watching a dog for one of the employees visiting her family. Jon thought I adopted her, but I set him straight. Be nice to her and don't pull any werewolf dominance shit. Okay?"

Pat looks indignant. "You know I love dogs, asshole. I wouldn't do that."

"Uh-huh," I say, unwilling to remind him I saw him growling at the biggest wolf hybrid in my pack of dogs before we left for Buenos Aries.

The wiry Were takes a seat at the table and props his feet up on the wood. "I know that look. Fuck off, you guys. I love dogs. And they love me."

"Where's the dog now?" Eric asks while looking under the table. "Do you have her crated somewhere?"

More of the tension drains from me. Maybe I can pull this off. I'm feeling crazy and dangerous for thinking it might work. Damn her. Why did she put me in this spot? "Last I saw her, she was with Vivian and Rafe."

"Really?" Pat says, eyebrows rising on his forehead. "Mistress Scary doesn't strike me as the dog type." He shoots me a look, a devilish grin on his face. "Present company excluded, of course." He winks. "She looks like a cat person to me."

Motion at the doorway draws our eyes. Vivian stands at the entrance with a smile on her face and the Pit Bull by her side. "And what does a cat person look like, Pat? Do they wear 'I prefer pussy' tee shirts or something?"

Pat's eyes go wide while the rest of the boys break out laughing at his expense. He recovers quickly, a humorous, smart-ass expression filling his face. "That would work, yeah. But it might lead to some confusion, too."

"I bet," Rafe says, appearing behind Vivian in the hall. His wife saunters in and takes a seat at the head of the table, the dog Asa supposedly adopted settling at her feet. Rafe takes the seat next to her, nodding hello to Eric and Asa.

"I've renamed your dog, Asa." The powerful vampire winks at him and then glances lovingly down at the animal she has no idea is Candy, my lover. "Miraposa." The dog's tale thumps against the carpeted floor. "She seems to like it better."

"She's not mine actually," Asa says, changing his story on the fly. "You can call her whatever you want. I'm fostering her for a friend who works with the local shelter in Fairbanks."

"Good! She's just the sweetest thing."

"Fostering? I thought you said you were watching her," Eric says.

Asa smiles. "It's kind of the same thing—but it means she doesn't have a permanent home yet."

"Oh, that's terrific," Vivian says, her face lighting up with joy. "Maybe if she works out well here we can keep her."

"I wouldn't mind having her in our suite," Rafe says. "But we don't have any food for her."

I clear my throat, hiding my discomfort as best I can. "I, uh,

I'll take her to the kennel with me when she needs to eat. I've got plenty of dog food."

"Nonsense," Rafe says, smiling adoringly at his happy wife. "Bring the food here. She's no trouble staying with us. Besides, Asa's already had her here for a while, no need to confuse her further with taking her to your place and introducing her to your pack of mutts."

I glare at the animal my girlfriend is pretending to be. "Fine. But she'll need exercise. I'll take her for a run after the meeting."

My two bosses nod, clearly happy the 'stray' will be staying with them. This can only end badly. What the hell is going to happen when the animal they've doted on turns into a woman? A woman who's doing the horizontal mamba with their right-hand man?

Holy crap. I'm screwed. Could this shit get any worse?

"Okay, back to the upcoming meeting. You two," Vivian says, indicating Eric and Pat with a pointed finger, "are here at Jon's request. He said you're now a part of our security team and need to know what we're up against. Speak up if you have something to add, but leave the sophomoric humor at the door."

"Yes, ma'am," Pat says, without a trace of his usual cockiness. Eric sits up straight and nods his assent.

Holy freakin' hell, it's like the unruly bastards are growing up right before my eyes. But then again, they both spent time in the military so they should be used to being serious when the situation warrants it. Attending a meeting with an ancient being certainly counts.

And just like that, the tone of the entire gathering changes. We wait until Drew and Paul arrive and then quickly get down to business, everyone listening while Rafe, Vivian, and I relay everything that happened in Buenos Aires and what it means to us and our future.

Looking like he's unable to hold his tongue any longer, Asa says, "I get the distinct impression we're on the verge of going to war. Only this won't be like any battle I've ever fought before. Instead of an entire army of trained men and women, we'll be a small, specialized squadron, kind of like a SEAL or Ranger team, against an unknown number of enemies." He looks around the table and nods. "I'm not liking the sound of those odds. But I understand we don't have a choice. Makes me extra glad we've started a weapons and martial arts training regimen with Paul and Drew."

Rafe clears his throat, his calm face appearing more serious. "The threat may never physically come here. We don't know. But it's always good to be prepared."

"Asa's right," I interject after he's finished, "but so is Rafe. The fight may not come here, but we, as in those not fully human anymore, we're about to face a serious threat to the entire existence of supernaturals. These whackos intend to subvert an entire city to their distorted perception of ancient Atlantis. Will they stop there or could their vision go global? You know humans will retaliate, as they should. What happens in Buenos Aires could essentially launch a war between humanity and supernaturals the world over."

Eric and Pat look a little green around the gills. Glad to know Asa's not the only one who realizes the seriousness of the situation. Drew doesn't look as shocked, but he was with us in Argentina a few weeks ago, maybe he suspected as much.

"We fear what's coming will completely change the current status quo on our secrecy. However things unfold, one thing is certain—our lives will never be the same again. " My words lie heavy in the room. "Thanks to Vivian and Rafe, this resort is the safest place any of us could be. We know the property and its defenses better than anyone on the planet."

"Agreed," Eric says, shaking off the weight of his fear, "it's easily defensible, especially with the advantage of the tunnels, and we're much harder to kill. But what about the human employees—are they in danger? Should they even be here if we're expecting trouble?"

Rafe sits forward in his seat, resting his forearms on the thick table. "Good questions, Eric. But we have no idea if Rolando and Persephone will come here or not. Evacuating the resort might be hasty at this point."

Asa looks pensive, as if he's turning an idea over in his mind. After a moment he speaks, "They can't be working alone. Do you have any idea who else is in on this with them?"

Rafe shakes his head. "No, we don't. They're the only two we know of so far, but we're sure they've turned their own share of manipulator vamps over the centuries. Why else would Coraline have tortured Vivian for what she knew about a secret manipulate group? There were obviously a few vampires worried about the possibility, even if their methods were aimed at the wrong vamps.

"No matter how you cut it, the odds are with Persephone and Rolando. Despite Vivian's assurance she was on their side, they don't trust her and didn't share any details of their master plan."

"Well, yeah, the lack of trust was obvious," Pat says, anxiety and anger pouring off him thick enough to smell. "You don't mind-rape people you trust."

Vivian's cool voice floats across the meeting space,

bringing calm assurance with it. "You're all right. The situation is deadly serious. We have no idea how many manipulators they've turned over the years, nor how many they've swayed to their idea. And they had a list of my turns."

Paul perks up, finally joining the conversation. "Holy shit. Does that mean they could be coming after me next?"

"You're safe," she replies. "For now."

"What the hell does that mean?" he says, partially rising from his seat, before realizing that in doing so he would be looming over his very scary boss. "Should I be worried or not?"

The redheaded vampire sighs, waving him back down, before beginning her explanation. "Vampires are required to report their turns to the Tribunal after the fledgling makes it to the one year mark. You aren't that old yet."

"And what happens then? You report me and then one of those crazy manipulator nut-jobs will come take me away to join their army of crazy?"

"No, Paul. I won't report you as a surviving turn. They'll never know you exist."

Relief spills across the chef's face.

Drew, who has been watching and listening, cocks his head to one side while speaking. "Aside from this current development with Persephone and Rolando, is there another reason you might not report Paul to the Tribunal?"

A small smile lights on our vampire master's face. "I can always count on you to nail down the details, Drew. To answer your question, yes, there is another reason." Her eyes settle on Paul, an appraising glint in their depths. "I believe there's a strong chance Paul carries my manipulator traits, and because of that, I would never have reported him at the one year mark, even if other manipulators weren't planning to come out of the closet very soon."

Drew sits back with a satisfied look on his face. "I knew it! When he snuck up on Emiko in the hangar and stabbed her, I knew he had to be doing something to hide himself from us both."

Paul shoots up from the table again, this time making it all the way to his full height, his pale complexion looking almost waxen in the conference room's lighting. "What the hell? I didn't do anything special. I swear it! I'm not a manipulator vampire. I just wanted to go unseen for a little bit."

Rafe motions with both hands for him to return to his seat. "Calm down, Paul. You're not a manipulator—yet. She's saying you're carrying the trait. What you did to sneak up on Emiko *unseen* is proof you may evolve into one over time."

"With practice and hard work," Vivian adds. "It's not an easy skill to master, trust me. Took me almost two decades. And I was coerced into using my skills daily."

Something she says triggers Asa to say, "You said the Tribunal has a list of all the vampires you've turned?" She nods. "Who else is on that list?"

Vivian looks to Rafe, an unprecedented show of unease flicking across her visage. "I'm not sure," she says. "It's an old list. There's only one turn from this century that I remember reporting."

"That you remember?" Paul asks, dismay over her phrasing showing in his expression. "Do I have a loss of memory to look forward to as well?"

She grimaces before answering. "No, nothing like that. I altered my memories, on purpose, by sheer force of will. Essentially, repeating over and over the lies I wanted to believe, to protect any manipulators I may have turned. And as far as I can tell, I also never reported them to the Tribunal."

Drew leans forward, matching Rafe's pose, his forehead creased in concern. "Does that mean there might be more manipulators like you running around, and you have no idea who or *where* they are?"

She sits back in her chair, her lids lowering halfway, and folds her arms across her middle. "Perhaps."

The room breaks into loud chatter, everyone vying to be heard at once. The predominant question of how she altered her memories is the one repeated the most. Reluctantly, the couple reveals what Dria did to protect the vampires she created and how the knowledge of her past lies hidden in her journals. Their names are only recorded in the journals, the ones casually stored in the couple's office on the main floor above us.

Rafe explains his desire to electronically scan the journals and perform a search for terms and phrasing in the digitized versions, speeding up their hunt for who they'll need to track down. Asa agrees to help with the scanning and they make plans to start immediately after the meeting.

Asa raises a hand slightly to call attention to himself. "Hey, guys, something you said about the list they have got me thinking. Did anyone see the list Persephone and Rolando had? You know, clear enough to read it?"

I straighten in my chair, knowing this aspect lies solely on my shoulders. "I got a quick look at it. But a lot of shit went down at that time and I wasn't studying it to memorize. I only recall that I was surprised some of the names on it were women's names."

Asa's forehead furrows. "Would Cy Whitfield be on the Tribunal's list of your recent turns?"

Rafe and Vivian look at each other for a moment, perhaps doing that silent communication thing they do, then Viv nods. "Yes, he'd be on the list. We should call to warn him."

"But you're sure you reported him, right?" Asa pushes to make certain.

"Of course. He showed great control over his blood lust and was on his own long before anyone else I'd turned. Why, Asa? What has you so worried?"

He looks a little sick to his stomach, but he forges ahead. "I think Cy tried to get into my head when he was here last."

My temper rises, do these idiots know nothing of communication? "And we're just hearing about this now? What the hell?"

He shrugs. "I wasn't sure if I was right. The sensation stopped as soon as I called him on it, and then he denied ever trying to mesmerize me. The incident started with simple questions, and then he attempted to press me." He motions with his chin to our master vamp. "He was very curious about you, Vivian. I refused to answer his questions, and he dropped the topic completely after I accused him of trying to of read my mind. I would have told you the moment you arrived if I'd thought the incident was vitally important, but I didn't think it was something I should relay over a phone call."

Concern crosses Rafe's face as he reaches for his wife's hand. "Is it safe to assume he could have been a late bloomer as far as manifesting manipulator traits?"

"I don't know," Vivian replies. "If you recall, I cut him loose way before the one year mark hit—wasn't it closer to three or four months? And thanks to changing my memories, I didn't think to look out for the possibility he could be a manipulator further down the line."

"How long does it normally take for the trait to manifest?" Drew asks.

"I'm not sure." Vivian's slim, pale fingers massage her right temple while she stares down at the table. She turns her head slightly to meet her husband's intense eyes. "Logically, signs would appear before the first year, right? Or how else would I have known to *not* report them at the one year mark to the Tribunal."

Rafe murmurs his agreement and several of us nod around the table.

She looks up, her clear green eyes holding a shadow of uncertainty. "Okay, then. That's a start. I could also have gone into their minds to try to discern if the ability was present."

I wonder if the time frame of *when* she changed them, meaning in relation to her own age and level of power, would come into play. "Could some of your turns have taken longer to show signs of the power?"

"You mean like how Rafe mentioned the possibility of Cy being a late bloomer?" The redhead lifts a shoulder in indecision. "Regarding latent vampire traits, I'm sure anything is possible."

Drew speaks up, "What about the opposite end of the equation, could other fledglings manifest the trait sooner than earlier turns? Specifically, how long was Paul a vampire before he projected his invisibility illusion to Emiko?"

Paul responds, "I think it was only a few weeks, right?"

"Yeah, that sounds right," Drew agrees with a nod.

A chill goes down my spine as a new thought occurs to me. "Conceivably, just like the powerful blood we sell in the bar, which is stronger as the vampire ages, Vivian's inheritable traits could have evolved as she aged. Which means a genetic tendency toward becoming a manipulator for each later turn would be increased."

Rafe picks up on what I'm saying, a gleam of interest in his eyes. "You're suggesting, in her older turns the trait may have presented itself or not, like a crap shoot, but as she aged and grew in power over the centuries, the chance of almost *every* turn becoming a manipulator would be much higher?"

A quiet settles in the room as the importance of our musings sink in.

Eric clears his throat before he speaks. "Why are we guessing? Why not just look in your journals?"

Rafe smiles, a mild look of wistfulness on his face. "Ah... we're hypothesizing because the knowledge is buried in over ten thousand handwritten pages in some very old books, that's why."

"Then we really should get on that, shouldn't we?" Eric asks. "I volunteer to help read them if you need it."

A chorus of volunteering sounds around the room before Vivian holds up a hand. "I appreciate you all wanting to help. But I hid this knowledge for a reason. Asa will help scan the data into a computer, but only Rafe will be permitted to read what's in the pages. I'm sorry, but we can't risk it."

Pat says, "Okay, I can respect that. Even though it would no doubt be fascinating and possibly scary as hell, I understand where you're coming from. But let's get back to the issue Asa mentioned with Cy. It sounds like he could have the traits. And you guys said he's on their list, right?"

I shift in my seat, clenching and unclenching one fist over

and over again. "I can't say for sure if his name was on the list. But it sounds like it would have been."

"I have an idea on how to discover if his name was there or not," Vivian says. "How about I go back into your memories and see if I can read who was on the list?"

"Will that work?" Paul asks. "Because if it will, I think there are some old recipes I've misplaced that I would love to know again."

"Another time, Paul." Vivian smiles and shifts her attention back to me. "It might work."

"Which is more important," Asa asks, "the names on the list and reaching them first, or finding out who *wasn't* reported to the Tribunal to begin with? Aren't the unknown vampires in your journal safe at this time?"

"Yes, for the most part. But if we plan to stop Persephone and Rolando from forming a new Atlantis, then we'll need manipulators on *our* side. There's no way I can stop them by myself."

Eric raises a hand. "Hold up for a second and bear with me. I know you guys already have this set in your heads, but I need to get a grip on it. So... The first focus is on the Tribunal's list. And then... after Rafe reads the journals, we'll work on finding the people Persephone and Rolando don't know about?"

A grimace forms before I can push it away. "Yes and no. We wanted you all informed of what was going on and to get your input. And yes, we'll need help in locating the people on the list the Tribunal has. But—and here's the 'no' part—the main task of physically tracking down the names in the journal will not fall to any of you, but to Rafe, Viv, and me."

Eric and Pat nod, but Drew and Asa look annoyed. Drew

turns out to be the first to voice his concerns. "You guys get to have all the fun and we're stuck here in the summer, hoping we don't singe and die from the never-ending sun."

Asa's annoyance lessens, like he wasn't thinking along those lines, but he doesn't respond.

The good humor Vivian showed all evening winks out, as if it was never there. "Would *you* rather face my unknown offspring and hope you can convince them to side with me, the absentee maker who has left them alone for decades or centuries? By all means, Drew, if you think you can do a better job than *me*, feel free. I would gladly stay here, safe and fortified, and wait for the danger to come to us." She leans closer, a deadly spark in her eyes. "When all is said and done, and the proverbial shit hits the fan, I *know* I'll survive. That's one thing I never doubt. But will *you?*"

Drew backs down, looking like he's swallowed a crow, no longer full of bluster. After a moment, our master vampire looks around the room, meeting the eyes of everyone individually, waiting to see if anyone else wants to speak out. She sits back and nods, apparently seeing what she thought she'd see.

What can you say when the most powerful person in the room calls you out, forcing you to admit you're not strong enough to handle the job? You silently take it, that's what.

"All right, gang," Rafe says after a moment. "You've all got the main gist of everything we know. Let's meet back tomorrow night to reconvene and report on where we are. Despite not allowing anyone to read the journals, we're all in this together and I want to keep the communication lines open."

"Jon," Vivian says as the I prepare to bolt out of the room. "Please wait for me in our office upstairs. I'll attempt to read the list from your memories before you head home for the night. Oh, and don't forget to bring us dog food in the morning," she adds with a smile, reaching down to stroke Candy's head again.

I nod in a jerky dip of my head and leave, followed closely by Paul and Drew.

Vivian's voice trails behind us. "Asa and Eric, could you stay for a moment please? There's something we'd like to speak to you both about."

CHAPTER THREE: ERIC

My stomach clenches, just like it used to in the Army when a commanding officer asked to speak to me. I never knew what the hell it was for at the time, the request always made me feel slightly off-kilter, and I would mentally run through everything I did recently to find fault.

Asa glances my way with raised eyebrows. I don't respond, having no idea what the two of them could possibly want with us.

When everyone leaves, even the lingering Pat, holding out for an invite, Rafe shuts the door. Asa's eyes widen a little in concern.

This doesn't look good.

Vivian waits for Rafe to return to his seat before speaking. "There's no easy way to say this, so I'll come out with it. We think we may have hired your brother, Justin."

Asa's brow furrows. "What's that now?"

"That makes no sense," I say. "How could you have hired

him? And why would you?" My head shakes in disbelief. "Neither of us even knows where he is."

The redhead nods. "If I was hearing it like this, I'm sure I'd feel the same way. I wouldn't believe the claim until I saw him with my own eyes."

"What makes you think the new hire is our brother?" I ignore the niggling in my gut reminding me our family name isn't all that common.

"He grew up in New Jersey, like you two did," Rafe says, "has two brothers he hasn't seen since he was a young teenager, he left the country with his mom fifteen years ago, and he's the name of the brother you two are missing—Justin Monson."

Asa's action mirrors mine from a moment before, and he shakes his head from side to side. Disbelief is apparently strong in both of us on this one. "Sure, it's not a common name. But come on." Thoughts tumble across his face, like he's trying to make sense of their claims. "You want us to believe you stumbled across him... where? At some airport on your way home from Argentina?"

Vivian reaches toward Asa, but drops her hand when she sees him pull back slightly from the table. I wonder what that's all about?

"He did security work in Buenos Aires for the vampires, as a wizard for hire. He helped Rafe when I was taken by Coraline, and he proved helpful again when we went back later to track Rolando."

Asa asks, "Isn't he the wizard you originally thought was the killer? The one that helped you piece everything together with the mythical creatures coming back to life?"

"Yes," she says. "I know it sounds crazy that we meet your

brother in such a roundabout way, but I've had odder occurrences happen in my life, trust me. Sometimes the Fates conspire to make things fall the way *they've* perceived. Other times it's dumb luck. I think this situation is a little of both."

"What about our mother?" I ask. "What ever happened to her? Did you find her, too?"

"I'm sorry to say," Rafe answers, "but according to Justin, she died in a house fire six years ago."

"And why didn't he try to find us when she died?"

"You'll have to ask him. Assuming we're right." Rafe glances between the two of us, drawing his phone from his pocket, and tapping the screen. "Have a look at this. Tell us what you think. It's his employee photo."

And there, in full color, is a mature version of the brother I never thought I'd see again. Older, more defined facial features, but there's no mistaking the mischievous glint in his eye I remember from childhood, or the familiar cowlick of hair near his forehead. "Well, holy shit. I think that's him."

After Vivian and Rafe drop the bomb on us about our brother, they leave. I hear them speaking quietly to each other as they ascend the stairs from the old workroom in the basement, which lies just beyond the command center's sliding wall door.

"What do you think?" I ask Asa as we join Pat, and settle into chairs in front of the wall of terminals. "Could it really be him?"

"There's no denying the picture looks like him," Asa replies, staring at a spot above the glowing screens.

"What are you guys talking about?" Pat asks, kicking back in his seat and propping his feet on the desk.

"Vivian and Rafe may have hired our long-lost brother."

"Justin?!? Get the fuck outa here. How? What are the chances of that happening?"

Asa raises his eyebrows and scratches his bald head. "According to Vivian, the 'Fates,' as she called them, often conspire to bring situations into alignment."

Pat's face scrunches in disbelief. "What kind of feel-good happy crap is that?"

I grab a squishy stress ball off the desk and toss it straight up, tracking its progress to catch it on the downward descent. "No idea, dude. Sounded like horse shit when she said it."

Pat leans forward, taking his feet off the wood and dropping them loudly to the floor. "But could it really be him?"

I toss the ball again. "No idea."

Asa's hand darts out and grabs the ball before it can land in my hand, tossing a self-satisfied grin my way. "Guess we'll find out tonight. Can you wait that long, or would you like to meet him when I'm sleeping?"

I can't stop the smirk from forming. "*Sleeping?* Is that what we call it now when you're literally dead to the world?"

"Screw you. Yeah, we're calling it sleeping. As in, the restorative sleep a vampire needs so he doesn't accidentally drink down his annoying little brother."

Jon walks in, a harried look on his face. "Just checking in on you two before I let Vivian into my head. How are you doing with this whole lost-brother-conveniently-appears-in-your-life-fifteen-years-later thing?"

A smile creases my pale brother's face. "Leave it to you to

pare the entire situation down to one odd sweeping generalization."

"Hey, I call 'em like I see 'em. But in all seriousness, I'd love to be able to have a relationship with anyone from my family. Count yourselves lucky." He shoves Eric in the shoulder. "As in very lucky."

"Lucky *if* it's him," I say. "If not, it's just some weird guy with our brother's name."

"Isn't that in essence who he'll be to us anyway?" Asa asks. "We don't know him now. We only have the distant past in common. He'll be a weird guy who does magic until we get to know him better."

"I remember those times," Pat says. "Justin always was a bit of a prick way back when."

Asa straightens and tosses the ball at Pat's head. "Come on, man. Is that really fair? He was put in charge of us when we were little and our mom couldn't be bothered. What we really needed was a babysitter to keep us in line, not a sibling too close in age to be respected."

Jon shakes his head. "So that's it? You guys have already accepted as truth that this guy is your brother?"

I look to Asa, whose expression remains stoically neutral, as usual, but I still feel as if I can read him like I used to as kids. And my gut is telling me, yeah... that's it. We trust that it's really him. Like Vivian said, Fate's a funny bitch. Or something like that.

I smile at our alpha. "Yeah, pretty much. Acceptance is like that, you know? Kind of makes the quirky weird stuff that's happened the past two years a little easier to handle."

Asa clears his throat and directs his next question to Jon.

"Speaking of quirky weird stuff, what were you babbling before the meeting—something about Rafe?"

"Oh, yeah," I nod. "What the hell was that?"

Jon looks toward the closed door, probably weighing whether or not the couple is listening to us. By my guess, they're upstairs now and we've got the sound-proofed, secure command center to keep our conversation private. We should be able to speak freely. "I think he's gaining vampire traits—as in more strength and mad skills. Like he's evolving to share more of Vivian's traits."

"Get out!" Pat says. "That would be some crazy-ass shit." He smirks and burps, pleased with himself, then scrunches his face up in disbelief. "Come on. Be real."

I snag the stress ball from the floor and aim it at Pat, who sees me and quiets. "Hold up, now. Don't dismiss Jon out of hand. He's known them for years. He would pick up on changes and inconsistencies a lot faster than we would."

Asa leans back in his chair, looking like he's contemplating what Jon said. "I think Jon may be on to something. I've noticed odd things along those lines, too. He's incredibly fast while sparring—like he's not fully human. And he hits like a freakin' tank. But as I haven't been here as long as you, I wasn't positive he didn't have the abilities before."

Pat's face takes on a pensive expression. "Okay, just for shits and giggles—what kind of other 'Vivian' traits is he manifesting, Jon?"

Jon rubs a hand on the table in a circle, not meeting our eyes. "I can't be sure, but I think he's developing the ability to mentally control humans."

"Snap!" Pat exclaims. "No shit?"

I shoot Pat a look, and ask Jon, "How can he manifest a vampire ability if he hasn't turned into a vampire yet?"

"My assumption is it's due to the blood he drinks from her. And that maybe he's been drinking more lately."

"Is there like a limit on how much a human should drink?" I ask.

Jon shakes his head. "I have no idea. That's out of my experience. I know there's lots of cases of vampires becoming addicted to wereblood and the crazy behavior that can follow. But as far as how much a human bonded mate *could* safely consume and not become an addict? I haven't a clue."

Asa glances away, toward the desk, and I wonder if he's thinking of Joanna, the crazed vampire he killed a few months ago, who wanted a steady stream of Vivian's blood. She tried to convince him they should capture and slowly drain our master vamp to increase their power. Needless to say, Asa is quite loyal, if a little quick on the draw. She's dead now due to her traitorous suggestion.

"We already know vamp blood can be addictive to vampires, too," Asa responds. "That's why the old ones are so careful with who they'll share with and how often."

"Should we be worried?" I press, tension tightening the muscles in my back and neck. "Should 'we,' meaning *you*, Jon, talk to Vivian about it?"

Jon shoots me a dirty look. "Oh, hell no. You really think me, or *anyone*, questioning an ancient vamp on what she does in private with her spouse is going to go over well?"

"Okay," I concede, "good point. So, what do you suggest?"

"How about we all keep our eyes and ears open and you guys let me know if you're ever worried about your safety, Rafe's, or anyone else's. I don't claim to understand all the nuances of their relationship, and truth be told, I have no experience with other vampires and bonded mate pairings to compare, but I think he's stable. As in, not likely to go bat shit and kill anyone."

Pat perks up, sitting straighter in his chair. "Hey, I just thought of something. Could he be a 'living-vampire'? Like a human-turned-vampire who hasn't died yet? I think I saw that term in a book once."

"Dude, you read?" I say with a grin. "I'm impressed."

My buddy flips me the bird in response. "Fuck off, man. I read and shit."

Jon appears thoughtful, ignoring our banter. "I don't know. But the theory of a living vamp is as good as any."

The sound of footsteps descending the old stairs reaches our enhanced hearing, soon followed by the slide of the concrete wall door, effectively ending the rest of our musings.

"Hi," Rafe greets us, laden with a big box full of books and an old flatbed scanner. He looks around at our little gathering and smiles while shoving his burden onto a clear stretch of desktop. "You ready for the mail run tomorrow, Eric?"

Pat and I have been taking flying lessons from Drew, and the weekly trips down to Fairbanks to collect mail, specialty food supplies, and other deliveries, has been great for accumulating the required flight hours to complete our license.

"Yes, sir," I reply as he draws a chair from the wall to join us. "The plane is already fueled up. We'll do our last pre-flight checks tomorrow morning and be in the air around nine."

Rafe picks up a book and examines the spine. "Good. Glad to hear it." He sets it back down and begins attaching cables to the scanner. "How close are you two to being finished?"

"I'm about three quarters of the way done." I look at Pat.

"You're about halfway?" He nods. "At the rate we're going, we should both be fully licensed before the snow hits."

"Great. That'll come in handy when the tourist season starts again and we need pilots for supply runs."

Jon edges toward the door. "I've got to get back to take care of the dogs, see you guys later."

"Hey," I say after looking around, "where is the pup? I didn't see her leave."

"Vivian called her up with us," Rafe replies. "Jon, can you check on her, see if she needs to go out?"

Jon's jaw clenches, and he takes a deep breath. "Sure. I'll run her and put her back in the kennel."

The werewolf quickly looks to Asa, his eyes widening, as if realizing what he said after the fact.

Rafe's forehead creases. "I thought she was staying with Asa?"

"Uh, yeah," my brother says without missing a beat. "But, er, uh, she's been fine with the other dogs, too." He refrains from saying anything else, as if it just occurred to him he might have stepped into the middle of an issue by talking about the new dog. I wonder what the issue might be.

Rafe picks up on it as well. "Am I missing something, guys?" He looks to each of us in turn, waiting for one of us to speak. "You know, regarding the dog?"

"No," the three of us say all at once.

Sure, that wasn't awkward or anything.

Asa tries to salvage the situation, as Jon looks like he's ready to scream and run from the room. "I didn't want to get too attached to her, knowing she'd be going back to her foster family soon anyway. So, it's no big deal to me where she stays. How about you, Jon?"

"She's a dog. She'll be fine. I've got to go. Get the dogs squared away. Vivian is expecting me." And with that, he walks out, effectively ending anymore conversation on the subject.

Geez, that's certainly one way to avoid a topic.

Boss man looks toward us for a second longer before nodding and says, "Okay." Then he returns his attention to the task at hand and begins to rifle through the old, musty books again. "Let's get started on these. Okay with you, Asa?" My brother nods and Rafe's gaze travels after Jon's exit. "I need to head back upstairs for something and I'll be back in a few."

"Yeah, sounds great, boss. Catch you two later, bros."

And with that, Pat and I are summarily dismissed. Well, it's late anyway. Might as well go see what what's on TV. Or maybe see who's on duty in the kitchen. I could always eat.

CHAPTER FOUR: VIVIAN

J on stopped in a moment ago, as requested, for me to read his mind on the list he saw in Buenos Aires, took one look at Asa's dog curled up at my feet and called her out of the office, saying she needed to go out before bed and he'd be happy to take her out. Maybe he's trying to get to know the animal a little better, I don't know, and frankly, I'm a bit too on edge to worry about his issues over a new dog on the resort.

My foot jiggles against the desk, creating a thumping sound, as I contemplate how to handle the upcoming situation. I need to delicately pick my way through Jon's mind, avoiding what he doesn't want me to see, while trying to respect his privacy as best I can.

Rafe enters, and takes a seat on the edge of the desk, glancing at my jittery foot.

"Really, darling? You're nervous about reading the mind of your werewolf servant?"

Frustration forms a grimace on my face before I purposefully push it away. "How can I not be? There's got to be a reason why he hasn't told us who he's involved with and why. That means both of us need to give the man some space." I smooth back my hair, tucking a loose tendril behind one ear, and will myself to stop worrying. "He's fine. I know it. That means I need to back off. Love won't blossom with a master vampire looking over your shoulder."

"So... you *are* nervous."

"Because it's important, dammit! I need to uncover what he knows regarding that damn list they had, and yet *somehow*, still avoid everything he's hiding that I desperately want to know. Trying not to reveal a private thought is worse than a bull in a china shop trying not to do damage, and is more like an innocent trying not to see boobs in a nudist colony."

"Do what you've always done. Don't anticipate trouble." He rubs a broad hand over my shoulders. "You've got this. Go slow and easy. There's no rush. We have all night."

My mind drifts to our bedroom down the hall. "Hopefully, not *all* night. I'd like to get reacquainted with our bed soon."

Rafe stills his hands and leans down to my ear. "Are you suggesting what I hope you're suggesting, or are you in need of a restorative sleep?"

I reach up and clasp his hand on my right shoulder. "Are you up for it, old man?"

"Old—" he starts in, as a knock sounds at the door.

"Come in," I call out, a smile spreading across my face. Jon opens the door and steps in, closing it behind him.

"I'm ready," he says in a low tone. "Go easy on me," he adds, with a smart-ass grin on his face.

"Puh-lease," I say with emphasis, dragging the sounds out. "Like I've ever messed around in your head and hurt you before."

He nods, traveling deeper into the room, to plop down on the soft leather couch. "True enough. You haven't." He winks at me. "Yet."

I stand and shake out the last of the tension in my legs. I can do this. I can slip into his brain and avoid looking at his deep, personal memories. Why is this so hard? I've had to go into people's heads all the time—for centuries—and plenty of them had secrets they wanted to keep from me, which I allowed. Just because you can read everything in a person's head doesn't mean you should.

Rafe projects privately to me, *Yes, but you didn't care about them or their petty secrets. This time you do. You care about the man and you care about who is tugging on his heart strings. You also care about his privacy. You respect him. You'll do fine.*

Thanks. I know I'm not myself lately. And self doubt is not usually in my wheel house. This is just another indicator of my being out of sorts after the silver torture.

And a clarification just occurred to me, easing my worry.

Jon hasn't seen his new love interest the past few weeks while we were gone, so anything dealing with her physically would take place before he saw the list Rolando and Persephone had in Buenos Aires. Which means I should be safe to access his recent recollections.

Reluctant to delay any longer, I take a seat next to the joke-cracking, nervous werewolf. Unlike me, his nerves are broadcast through his scent and his poor attempts at humor. Even if he looks calm, cool, and collected, he stinks of sour anxiety and nerves. Granted, it's a subtle stink, but any supe worth their salt would pick up on it.

"Relax, Jon. You know this won't hurt."

"Relax? Why wouldn't I be relaxed?" He titters, a tiny awkward sound escaping him. "Of course, I'm relaxed."

"Uh-huh," Rafe says, taking my recently vacated seat behind the desk. "How about I'll write down the names as you call them off?" He reaches for the lined yellow pad on the far side of the desk.

I settle back into the deep cushions of the couch and reach out a hand to clasp one of Jon's. "Sit still. Take a deep breath and close your eyes. Don't try to guard your thoughts. I'll do my best to respect your privacy."

The jumpy werewolf nods, performing one last audible gulp before closing his eyes.

His warm fingers lie beneath my cooler ones, emitting a twitch before lying motionless.

I follow my own advice and take a deep breath, releasing it as I push my consciousness toward him, slipping easily into his familiar mind.

Instantly, I'm bombarded with images of the new dog Asa's caring for, but they're all tinged with anger and annoyance as well. Huh. I wouldn't have thought an employee getting a dog without checking with him first would leave such a strong impression on his mind. Unwilling to waste time, I push past the recent images and plunge deeper, sliding back toward the night in Rolando's apartment, where the evil dynamic-duo plundered my mind like a bunch of kids would a bowl of Halloween candy left out on a porch.

His memories of seeing me incapacitated and in pain are disturbing, as are his fear and emotions intertwined with the memory. I steel my resolve and slow down, examining each moment in a slower than real speed, so as not to miss the moment the list is visible to Jon's eyes.

After a few minutes, my diligence pays off. I start rattling off names, hearing the scratch of pencil on paper indicating my husband is taking notes. The last name is no surprise; it's Cy's. And now that we know he tried to crack into Asa's head the last time he was here, it means he's in danger.

I pull my awareness back, and carefully extricate myself from his sense of self and his mind. The couch dips next to me and Rafe touches my thigh to ground me.

"You did well, hon. Forewarned is forearmed."

I release Jon's hand and pat Rafe's hand resting on my leg. "Yes. It is. Let's have a look at those names."

"Did you get it?" Jon asks. "I think I drifted off to sleep for a little bit there."

I give him a warm smile, grateful I was able to respect his privacy and not dig into his mind to discover who he's been dating. "You done good, kid."

Rafe hands the pad to me and I scan the names. "Dead. Dead. No clue on this one," I say, pointing to a woman's name I vaguely recall from two centuries ago. "Or these two. Another Dead. And as I'd feared, Cy Whitfield. Dammit. What are the chances they've already gone after him?"

"Wouldn't we have heard something from him if trouble came his way?" Jon asks.

Rafe taps the notebook on his knee, my earlier feelings of anxiety obviously passed to him now that the task is over and we have the data we needed. "Not necessarily. What if he was taken unawares?"

"Then we'd have heard from Cali," I remind him.

"What if they were both taken?" Jon presses, unwilling to let it go.

I shrug. "There's no way to know exactly what Persephone

would have done—or if they wanted him dead or alive. Rather than sit here and guess what type of ill could have befallen my last turn, why not call him and warn him?"

"On it," Rafe says while reaching for the phone. After he picks it up, he checks the clock on the wall. "Shit, it's past dawn in New York. And I bet Cali isn't awake either." He hangs up and makes a note on his pad. "I'll call him again later today, and if I don't reach him, I'll have Asa follow up."

"Okay," I say, releasing the tension inside me. "That's at least a step in the right direction. Let's get these other names to Asa and see what he can uncover."

Rafe nods, taking his notebook with him when he stands. "Are you bringing food back here for Mariposa tonight, Jon?"

The werewolf immediately tenses and I have to hold back the urge to press him for what's wrong. Why is he reacting so strongly whenever we mention this dog? What is he hiding? A thought occurs to me, but I dismiss it. We'll just have to wait and see.

"Uh, I wasn't planning on it," he says. "It's late. I'm sure Asa fed her before we even landed. I let her out before, to do her business. More than likely she'll head back to the kennel with the other dogs. I'll, uh, bring the food over tomorrow."

And with that, he bolts out of the office. I don't know what's up with him, but since I haven't been myself lately, it's probably best we give him space and let him work it out on his own.

"That was weird," Rafe says. "Should we be worried? The guys downstairs acted odd about the dog before."

"Really? Huh. What about?"

"Nothing in particular that I could say. Things just felt *off.* They all answered a question at once, with the same answer—

and unless that was planned, it made me think they were hiding something."

"Could be because I renamed her and haven't made much of a secret that I'd love to have her for our own."

"I doubt it. How would that lead to them all speaking at once?"

"Awkward men who can't communicate their thoughts and feelings well?" I sigh. "It's our first night back. Let's give it a rest for now, what do you say?"

"Agreed." Rafe wiggles his eyebrows. "Besides, I'll be keeping you warm tonight. We don't need a dog in the bedroom with us."

A warm glow of anticipation flows through me. "Sounds good to me."

He trails both hands up and down my arms, but his face looks preoccupied, like he's deciding to broach a difficult topic. "There's something I want to talk to you about."

"Okay," I say with an encouraging smile, hoping it's a dirty thought followed by some dirty action. "Go ahead."

"I'd like to recommit our mate bond. Do the entire ritual again."

Surprise lights my face. "Really? So soon? We recommitted ten years ago. And even that's an oddity as far as I know. Most bond rituals occur once and then never again. Why now?"

He firms his grip on my biceps, squeezing once, then releasing me, tucking his hands in his pockets. "If it wasn't for the blood exchange we did the night Coraline ambushed us, I'd be dead."

A shudder runs through me. "I know. And I'd have soon followed, I have no doubt."

He nods, looking away. He understands what I hide from others, even if he'd rather not talk about it again. I'd rather end my long existence than face living without him. "That exchange saved me. Your blood helped me to heal. And our bond helped keep you alive during the silver torture. I need to make sure we're as strong as we can be for what lies ahead."

"Uh-huh," I say, still unsure why a recommitment of our mate bond matters so much to him right now. "Isn't that why we hired a wizard to teach you magic?" Could he be stressing about what's to come, and this is his way of planning for every conceivable result?

"Yes, but that was more like continuing education for a long-term result, not an immediate solution for our current situation. Did you really think I expected to be able to learn enough before the proverbial shit hits the fan with what we're up against?"

"I'm glad to hear you have realistic expectations. I'd rather not count on anything too new to save us when we need it."

"Agreed."

The memories of our last ritual flood my mind, snapshot-like naked images of us rolling around in orgasmic bliss for hours on end flash across my consciousness. Damn, this is going to be a nice bright spot of fun I wasn't expecting. Seven whole days of sucking and fucking. What more could a horny, power-hungry vampire ask for?

Oh, I know, a private bungalow somewhere, like last time, so we'd have no interruptions. And no obligations. The ritual feels like a dream honeymoon for a vampire. God, our week in the islands was heaven. Peaceful. Quiet. Just the two of us. It felt like we were the only two souls on earth. Since a recreation of that scenario is not an option at the moment, I'll settle for wild, blood-filled sex every day—no problem.

The power surge experienced during a mate bond makes for a potent aphrodisiac. Warmth floods my mid-section, trailing downward to the juncture between my thighs. Holy crap, I think my panties are damp. Me! The woman who experienced sexual satiation on the plane home only a few short hours ago. I obviously have no problem becoming aroused again so soon.

Damn, I love that man.

I draw away and take a seat on the couch, patting the cushion next to me, an inviting smile stretching my face. "I have no idea what's in store for us in the coming weeks, but only a fool would turn down a chance to reconnect and strengthen our ties."

"Good," my husband says, looking like a weight has been lifted from him. He notes my sexy, come-hither expression and smiles. "Hold that thought. Let me go check on Asa. Get him started on the journal scanning, and then I'll be right back."

He opens the door and strides down the hall toward the basement entrance just off the kitchen.

"Huh. I think I just got rain-checked on having sex." A devilish thought occurs to me. "I'm going to make him want it really, really bad."

I chuckle as I walk to our bedroom, stripping my clothing as I go.

CHAPTER FIVE: RAFE

I rush down the stairs, eager to get Asa started, so I can race back up to be with Dria. Her agreement to the idea immediately stirred an eagerness I haven't felt in a while. Despite this being a really stressful time for all of us, we'll have a way to work off that stress together and strengthen our ties at the same time.

After a few minutes, I've relayed our meeting with Jon to Asa, and passed on the information we uncovered. Asa's going to research the names from the Tribunal's list and see what he can uncover, but only after he's gotten a jump on scanning the journals. He didn't appear too hopeful when I told him some of the names were from over a hundred years ago.

"Are you sure you want to get started right away?" I ask while settling the first stack of leather-bound journals on the long table. "We dropped a lot on you with the possibility of a long-lost brother and I'd completely understand if you want to deal with that situation first."

The young soldier dips his chin in thanks. "Appreciate it,

boss man, but the knowledge in the journals is time sensitive for the next leg of this plan, right? Time is something we don't have much of if I'm understanding the scope of the threat correctly. And despite me wanting to work as long as I can, I'll be asleep for the day by four a.m."

At my raised eyebrows, Asa adds, "Vivian spiking the bagged blood helps us stay awake, don't get me wrong, but the effects don't last forever against the natural pull of the sun for a restorative sleep." He smiles, possibly to show he's sincere in the offer to work first. "And besides, if he really is my brother, I don't need to barge in on him this late for an unexpected reunion. How about if we arrange something for tomorrow night, after Eric gets back from the mail transport and I have a chance to wake up?"

I nod. "Okay, as long as you're sure."

"Yeah," he says while reaching for the first journal. He flips open the cover, pausing when he catches sight of the date. I look over his shoulder to see what made him hesitate.

May 15, 1451

"I can't even fathom being around for a hundred years let alone living for over five centuries," he says. "Insane."

The black ink has faded only a little on the thick paper. My wife's precise handwriting fills the page, easy to read, teasing me with the desire to see what she felt was important enough to keep record of.

"Does it matter which one we start with?" he asks.

"Obviously, it would be thorough of us to start with the oldest ones. But Viv claims she didn't sire any vampires the first seventy years or so. Something about hiding a lot and trying desperately to survive unnoticed by her fellow undead. Not to mention learning to master her manipulator skills on the down low. I got the impression she isolated herself from her kind for a long time."

"What if she's remembering wrong?"

My eyebrows creep up. "That's a viable point. She could be. We'll cross that bridge when we get to it. How about you start with scanning the journals with dates after fifteen-hundred, and then create a file named with the start and end dates contained on the first and last pages? After you complete the first one, I'll launch a search in the file for words and phrases that may point me in the right direction."

He nods and looks through the stack, selecting one with a start date of 1503. After lifting the lid on the flatbed scanner I brought down earlier, he carefully spreads the ancient journal open to lie flush on the glass surface and scans two pages at one time. Once the first pages are captured, he turns the page and scans again. The job is easy, but time consuming.

It takes him almost a half hour to finish the first book. Twice during the process, I felt Dria's presence in my mind. Like she was checking to make sure Asa stuck to the job at hand and didn't indulge in reading any of the entries. She always has had trust issues.

Once he compiles all the scans and converts them into a document with searchable text, he sends it to me via email. "One down. Forty-nine more to go," he says with a mock grimace. This is going to be time consuming job. "At this rate, and considering I have limited waking hours this time of year, I think it'll take me at least three days."

"Duly noted. You get started on the next one and after I look through this first file, I'll see about commandeering another scanner. No reason why I can't help with scanning, too."

I settle into a chair in front of one of the terminals, and open the document he sent. After scrolling through for a few minutes, I grab a notebook and start taking notes.

Asa sees me writing and looks like he can't resist the curiosity pulling him. "Find anything?"

"There's a list of what I can only assume are 'rules' she made up at some point."

"Oh, really?" Asa says, his eyebrows creeping up his forehead. "Care to share?"

I shrug, unable to see the harm in sharing something so small. "It's probably nothing you haven't already heard from her, I'm sure." I read the list aloud. "One, never turn a witch. Two, never turn a child. Three, never turn your mate," my voice hesitates on the last one. I hadn't expected to see a rule on never changing your bonded mate. We've talked about it a lot and she's open to turning me when the inevitability happens. "And the last one: Four, never lose control during a feeding."

Silence hangs between us for a moment while we both digest her words.

"Believe it or not," Asa says, "she didn't cover any of those with me, and neither did my maker or Cy. Cali told me the horror of changing a child, and how they never grow physically or mentally beyond a certain point. Apparently, if you change them too young, the result can become a pint-sized and blood-crazed sociopathic killer."

"That makes sense." I grimace. "And paints an utterly horrible picture." I turn back to the job and create columns on the yellow paper.

"Anything else in there that's safe to share?"

"No idea. I'm starting a timeline with names, dates, and

places mentioned. Figured it might come in handy as I continue."

He nods while continuing to scan pages. A name I've never heard before jumps out at me from the text. Finnegan. Huh. I read a bit further and shake my head. It's a good thing I've never been the jealous type. Especially when I discover another former husband I didn't know about.

Pushing the discovery out of my mind to deal with later, I decide to return upstairs to seduce my wife into starting the mate bond ritual again. There will be plenty of time to read these pages when I'm hyped up from our blood exchange.

I may not have been her first husband, or even her second. But, Fates willing, I will be her last. Nodding to Asa, I leave the command center and make my way back upstairs.

The aroma of vanilla drifts down the hall. There's a flickering light as well, coming from our bedroom. Intrigued, I follow my nose and my heart.

I cross the threshold of our bedroom with my heart thudding loudly in my chest. Tall, short, round and square candles line the room's every surface. Their warm glow the our illumination.

Dria lies in a silk robe, reclined against the headboard, a sensual smile curving her lips. Between us stands the small round table where we normally sit and enjoy coffee. On its surface, she's spread out a beautiful tapestry, one with swirling designs and geometric patterns combined. I'm not sure where she got it, but she's used it before when we've had a ritual. And judging by the chalice and silver knife laid so innocently on its surface, she's ready for us to begin our mate bond.

My pulse quickens as a smile draws the skin tight across my face. "So, I take it you want to jump right in?"

A rich, seductive chuckle spills into the air. "You asked. I agreed." She sits up. "You're right. It's a good idea." Her eyebrows wiggle. "Am I saying all the things you want to hear so you'll get naked?"

I grab my shirt hem and pull the fabric over my head, tossing the material toward the club chairs Dria has pushed against the walls. "You'll get no argument from me."

I step closer, my eyes landing on the cup and knife laid out on the fabric. To my surprise the cup is not empty, but is filled halfway with a dark red liquid that can only be one thing.

"Did you start without me?"

"I didn't start without you, per se. But I thought it wise to get the ritual started." She stands, the green silk robe delicately hugging her curves. She joins me by the table, and links her hand with mine. "Say the words with me, my love."

She picks up the fancy chalice on the table and holds it between us. I lock gazes with her, seeing a portion of my own soul reflected in her eyes as she stares back.

With a slight nod of her chin, she opens her mouth to speak, and the words rush unbidden to my lips as I repeat along with her, "My life is your life, the blood in our veins will bind us for all eternity. There is no beginning, there is no end, there is only one. We combine to make a bond that is unbreakable, binding your soul to mine."

As before when we'd done the ritual, each and every time, I feel a tingle along my nerve endings. It's not magic, well not magic in the truest sense of the word. But there are lots of energies swirling around—energy in the air, energy between us, and energy that binds us. And no matter what you call it, magic, woo-woo, or just good thoughts, whatever the hell it is, is real and I feel it. I feel it with her. I feel every moment of our lives coalesce between us, to become a real living thing.

"Drink of me, my love, gain strength from me. Like I do from you." Dria's eyes appear slightly damp, as if the emotions she's feeling fill her as mine do for me.

I take the goblet from her grasp, and even knowing exactly what's inside and what the taste will be, I still drink. As the glass touches my lips and the tang of iron from her blood crosses my tongue, I swallow it down never hesitating. Never stopping. Drinking down the lifeblood that runs through my wife's veins, knowing her eternal life is bound to my mortal one.

The warmth and viscosity of the liquid doesn't disgust me as it used to. It no longer scares me as it did the first time. I know now what true power is. As her strength seeps into my body, I feel her—her life, her energy—become one with mine. Her vitality flows through my veins, pulsing to my muscles, filling my head with wonderment, and confusing my senses with the brilliance of the room around me.

The candles glow brighter, their subtle heat a warm breeze against my skin. My jeans, snugger than usual with the blood rushing toward my cock, now feel even tighter.

"Your cheeks are flushed, Rafe. I bet you're starting to feel toasty in all my favorite places."

"How would you like to proceed?" I motion toward the knife on the table. "Do you want to drink from the glass as well?" One eyebrow quirks up sardonically, I know she doesn't want to drink of me from a cup. I know what she wants. But do I make her ask for it? That could be fun. Or do I simply give her what she wants?

"Don't go playing coy with me now. I can read your mind.

Do you really question what I want? Do you really wonder what I want to feel? Or is that you've always known, because of our bond?"

No. She's right. I do know what she wants. And it's not due to the vivid images coursing through her mind. They are colorful and filled with erotic detail. No, I know what she wants, because it's what I want. I want to make love to her all night long. I want our bodies to join and flow as one, just as our blood soon will.

Without another word, my hand goes to the top button of my pants. Her eyes dart down, taking in exactly what I'm doing. I watch her every moment, gauging her reaction, feeling what she feels as her blood pounds through my veins. The stiffness of my aching cock hammers its need behind my fly, straining to get out, straining to be exactly where I want. Which will be deep inside my wife.

Her tongue darts out and licks her lips. She reaches out to touch me. And draws back, almost as if remembering she wanted to tease me more. To *not* succumb to my desires as quickly as she might want to. Seems she's forgotten I can read her mind, too.

I separate the fabric at the top of my pants, and my zipper eases down, seemingly of its own accord, but it's more that the jeans are well-worn and the zipper knows its path. Tight black boxers conceal the engorged length of my prick. Seeing her not give in to her desires pushes me to be even more bold than I normally am.

I ease my jeans down over my hips, stopping at my thighs, allowing the fabric to trap my legs. The tight underwear showcases the round, dark-pink head of my cock pushing above the elastic waistband.

"You know what you want, Dria. How long are you going to resist?"

"You like to tease, don't you?"

I shrug, the action drawing her gaze from my crotch to my exposed bare chest. With her blood pumping through me, our bond is even greater, allowing me to slip into her mind as easily as she would slip into mine. Normally, I can only get this close to her thoughts when she's sleeping. When her guard is down. When she is open.

Every time we've experienced the mate bond ritual we end up closer than ever. Closer than she may like. But never close enough for me. Every fiber of my being is intertwined with hers—I can feel her hesitation. She's refusing to allow herself to reach forward and touch my bare flesh.

The desire for me boiling in her body is a seedy rush of power in my head. She wants me, all of me, every inch of me sliding into her, she wants my mind and hers to be one, just as our bodies are—or as they will be very soon if I have my way.

"Dria, why do you resist the pull inside yourself? You know you can always take me whenever you want. I'm putty in your hands, my love."

A flash of despair flits across her mind, squashed before she allows it free rein. Where does the despair come from, what worries her? Unwilling to allow any of our outside stresses, any of the problems we're facing, to come between us, I decide to take her choices from her. To force her desires to the surface.

I reach into my underwear and haul out my swollen length, lowering the fabric until it supports my balls, pushing them up on display. Unwilling to beg for her touch, I stroke my own flesh, pumping one roughened fist up and down, watching as my wife's laser sharp focus zeroes in on my every stroke.

"Where do you want it, baby?" I ask. "Do you want to touch it? Or do want it in your mouth?" My own breathing becomes rough as I continue to stroke my flesh. "Do you want to feel me deep inside your pussy?"

The power rushing through my veins feels heady. I know I can take her all night. Over and over again. I will make her scream and writhe in pleasure.

Her thoughts meld with mine. Enticing me to stroke a bit faster. She's waging an internal battle of whether or not she wants me to finish this way. Whether or not she wants to watch me reach completion, shuttering and moaning my pleasure through my own efforts, because watching me touch myself turns her on—or whether she wants to bring me off on her own.

"Or maybe, just maybe, what you really want is me pushing gently into your ass?" I grin as her breathing hitches. "Don't worry. You know I can eventually make it fit." Her mouth opens in a small little O of surprise. Glancing down, I see what has triggered her response. Moisture weeps from the slit of my cock, tempting her to lick and suck it, to draw the salty goodness into her mouth.

With her blood strengthening me, it's like a triple dose of Viagra winding me up all night. I know from past experiences I'll be able to reach multiple releases, my cock never softening all night.

I smile as her hidden thoughts come to me. "You're a bad girl, Dria. You want it all, don't you?" Yes, yes, she does. I can feel it in her mind, she desires everything I mentioned. My slick dick cramming down her throat, my flesh slapping against her hips as I pummel deep inside her moist heat, ohh... and then the tight, silky confines of her ass as I slowly slip back and forth in forbidden bliss.

"I will give it to you all, my love. Everything your heart desires." My wife meets my gaze and smiles.

Her sharp canines have elongated, and her eyes bleed black with desire. "Oh yes, I want it all. And I will have it."

And with that, she leaps, her body slamming into mine and staggering me back a step. Her midsection flattens my cock against my stomach, as she reaches up on tip toes to drive her teeth into my neck. I hold her close as pleasure spills throughout my body from the wound. The ritual words spill from my lips as they did before I drank her blood.

"My life is your life, the blood in our veins will bind us for all eternity. There is no beginning, there is no end, there is only one. We combine to make a bond that is unbreakable, binding your soul to mine."

CHAPTER SIX: JON

After running for a half hour to calm down, I storm into the cabin, my face still hot with anger and indignation, and slam the door shut. Candy sits on the couch in the small living room, her face composed and unreadable.

"What the hell do you think you're doing, pretending to be a goddamn dog to a master vampire? Were my instructions to stay in the cabin so repellant, you had to find something more *fun* to do?" My arms wave around while my voice gains in volume, my eyes widening in desperation. Guess that run didn't help as much as I'd hoped. "Jesus, Candy, she could kill you with a freakin' *thought*. Why couldn't you just wait?"

I stalk over to Candy's position on the couch, practically looming over her in my agitated state. Her long, dark wavy hair, lean strong body, and uncluttered beauty call to me, reminding me of how much I've missed her the past few weeks. It requires work on my part to resist the urge to take her in my arms and kiss her senseless—especially when my first instinct is to shake her for her recent actions.

A goddamned dog! What was she thinking?

"Hi, honey," she says, keeping her voice level and quirking up an eyebrow, like she's talking to a crazy person or something. "Good to see you, too."

"Don't 'hi, honey' me. What the hell game are you playing?"

Her face changes quick-fire, her mouth turning down and her expression closing. That's one way to tell me she doesn't like my tone or my words. I'm stepping onto tricky ground, and I know it. But dammit, doesn't she realize the danger she's put herself in?

"Are you done?" she asks, reaching up to twist her necklace between her fingers.

"With what?"

"Are you done yelling at me? 'Cause one thing I know for sure—I don't have to have to put up with *anyone* talking to me like that."

Did she really think we'd be talking about this bullshit quietly and calmly? "Like *what*? Like I care about what happens to you?" I turn from her and begin to pace the tight confines of the cabin. It's an energy-releasing habit I know I picked up from tiny, scary, and bitchy, but I can't help myself. The movement helps keep control of my inner wolf. "Like I worry for your safety—especially when you heedlessly put yourself in harm's way with an incredibly powerful, and volatile, vampire? Am I supposed to meekly sit back and never voice concern over your actions?"

"News flash, bucko: I survived a long time on my own before meeting you. Give me some credit."

"Really? Credit for what, hiding in the shape of a man while living in a werewolf pack? You shift form and think that makes you safe? Is that the same logic you applied to changing into a dog and cozying up to Vivian?"

"Give me a break. Just because I did things in my past, or present, different than you would, doesn't make it wrong or dangerous. Have you thought through what will happen when she finds out?"

"Of course, I have!" I stop pacing and turn to face her. "That's why I'm so pissed off you've pulled this stunt."

She tilts her head to the side and looks at me, making me stare into the brown eyes I've missed and wish I could drown in. "What do you think will happen, Jon?"

"I think she's going to be fucking pissed you lied and pretended to be a dog."

"No, Jon, that's not what I'm talking about. What do you think will happen when she finds out about *us*, about you and me sleeping together? Having a relationship? Or how about me living here in *your* cabin on *her* property? A stranger, cozying up to her *vampire servant?*"

"I... Uh..." I look away, annoyed I don't have an answer at the ready. "Truth be told, I don't know exactly what will happen. I've never been in this situation before, but I can guarantee it would have gone smoother if you hadn't made her fall in love with a freakin' dog she'll never get to keep."

She brushes off my words about Vivian falling in love with a dog. "I'll tell you what will happen. Are you listening? Really listening and not ready to fly off the handle again?" I reluctantly nod, doing my best to curb the raging temper and control my inner beast. "If you and I become a permanent item, she's going to *insist* I swear my loyalty to her—and more than likely, she'll do that with a blood bond. Immediately.

She'll make me her vampire servant just like you. Anything else could leave her open to danger down the line. And she knows it."

I stare down at the woman I've resisted admitting to myself that I'm falling in love with, and really *see* her sincerity and worry. She's afraid, too. But brave enough to try something crazy because I matter to her. All at once, my anger leaves me. She's right. Dammit. I may not agree with her methods, but she could be reading the situation correctly.

Vivian might very well not give her a choice. She may make her submit to a bond immediately. Especially at a time like this, when our enemies are actively seeking more soldiers. I don't want to think about it. And maybe that's my problem. I haven't wanted to think about the consequences. I've been too busy trying to see if what we have is real.

Unhappy with the distance separating us, I sit on the couch next to her, and try to pull her close with one arm. "Hey, that may not be what she does."

She chuckles, a mirthless sound if there ever was one, and I can feel the tension inside her as she resists my embrace. "You can continue drinking that Kool-Aid of delusion all you want, but I bet you *my life* she'll bind me to her."

I rub a hand across her shoulder blade. "Being bound to her isn't so bad. She's a kind person under the pointy teeth, red hair, and flashy clothes. She's been exceptionally careful with me and has never tried to take my free will."

"But you had a choice in the initial bonding, didn't you?"

"Yes, of course. If anything, I kind of pushed her into it." At her raised eyebrows I add, "That's a story for another time. But you'd have a choice. I'm sure of it."

"Hah! Yeah, sure. I'd have a few minutes to decide my fate

—maybe. If I was lucky." She adjusts on the cushion, turning to face me. "I needed to get to know her, Jon, on my own terms—before I make a choice that could affect the rest of my life."

"Wow, that's kind of heavy when you put it like that."

"Now add in the fact we've only known each other for a month. Would *you* be so eager to blindly sign over your freedom, blood, and possible sanity, without some kind of hands-on background information first?"

Considering the time we've known each other is probably exactly why I didn't examine the consequences too closely, I opt instead to address why she's behaving the way she is. "Is that what you're doing? Playing as a dog in some misguided attempt at research?"

"*Playing?!*" she shouts, pulling from my lingering touch and standing up to tower over me. "I was in disguise. This is not a game to me. Not at all. This is my future. And I resent you thinking I'm trying to play a damn game.

"Do you have a better idea for getting close to someone you don't know, who could kill you in a blink, but you want to get to know them, somehow, without their knowledge? Frankly, I thought the plan was rather ingenious. How else could I be near enough for her to let down her guard and have a chance to get to know her?"

"Come on! Do you really think tagging along as a dog will help you 'get to know her?' Don't kid yourself—she's not human, and normal rules don't apply. She's a manipulative, dangerous, and deadly creature. What is there to get to know?"

"You just said she was kind! And I have learned valuable information on my own already—she also loves animals, she's loyal, protecting who and what she loves, and she's just the type of person you want on your side in a fight. She's not some self-centered, power-hungry, killing machine like a few of the other vampires I've known."

"That's right, you've said you have experience with vamps before. That's how you knew to give me advice when we had the big game hunt here this spring."

"Yes. I knew if you and I were going to make it past a few months I'd have to commit to your master. And that's a big step. She may be reasonable about letting me leave if you and I don't work out, but I bet it would only happen if I agreed to a mind-wipe."

"You really think you'd have any choice in 'agreeing'? If a master vamp doesn't want you to know something, you can pretty much bet your life that you won't know it for long."

"Dammit, Jon," she says, her voice rising with her intense feelings. "That's precisely my point! How could I assess my risk if she was expecting me? How could I see what type of person she is underneath the mask of leadership and power if she reined in her behavior to *not* scare off her servant's potential mate?"

Mate.

My heart stutters in my chest.

Wow. Did she say *mate*?

Could this thing between us really be real? Could I have found someone for the rest of my life? Could we lead a pack together? I want her in my life more than I've wanted anything in a good long time.

I wait a moment, unsure how to respond. This could be more than I ever dreamed possible.

"What?" she demands, uncertainty blooming on her face over my silence. "Did I say something else to piss you off? Or maybe you would prefer a mindless bimbo who can't think for herself?"

A soft smile crosses my face. "Do you really think we could be mates?"

"*Of course,* I think we have a possibility, you dolt." She returns to the couch and sits close to me, grabs my face in both hands and stares into my eyes. "Do you really think I would have stayed here once I learned you belonged to a master vampire if I didn't think we could have a *real* future together?"

My arms wrap around her, drawing the sexy shifter close and squeezing hard, a squeak of surprise emitting from her. I nestle my mouth between her head and shoulder, planting a soft kiss on her neck. I drift further up her necklace and my lips singe in pain.

I draw away and stare at her necklace. "Are you wearing silver? What the hell?"

"I've had this on for weeks, didn't you notice it before?"

"I guess I never kissed it by accident. How can you wear silver?"

"Shape-shifters don't react to silver. Our issue is with copper. In addition to it burning us like silver does for Weres, it's antibacterial properties inhibit our ability to hold another form. Didn't you know that?"

"If you're the first shifter I've known, how would I know?"

She nods in agreement. "Okay, good point. Sorry I didn't tell you sooner. I'll take it off."

As she reaches up to remove it, I halt her hands. "Leave it."

"Really? I don't want to hurt you by accident."

"It obviously matters to you, where did you get it?"

"My parents gave it to me. A long time ago."

"Then that's even more reason you should keep wearing it."

She shakes her head, and pulls her hands free, reaching for it again. "I can easily put it back on when we're done." She kisses my mouth lightly while slipping the chain from her neck and putting it aside. "I'd rather not burn these delectable lips. They do good work."

I laugh and draw her close, the happiness inside bubbling to get free. "Good to know." I resume kissing her neck, stopping between each one to whisper. "I've dreamed of finding someone to spend my life with." My breath hitches with emotion, and I push past it. "For too many years, I feared I'd always be their third wheel."

Her arms shift to embrace me, one hand moving up and down in a soothing motion across my broad shoulders. "Oh, honey, she's a good woman. She never took your heart and used you. She left you free, at least as much as she could, for you to find your own happiness. From what I've seen and heard from you and others, she's a fair person. Her primary focus appears to be safety—that of her husband, the inn, and the seethe." A soft chuckle escapes her. "And she's got a soft spot for dogs."

I pull back and gaze into her eyes. "That's another thing. How did you know to pick a Pit Bull?"

"I saw an old black and white picture of Viv and Rafe posing with a Staffie in their office. A Staffordshire Bull Terrier is kind of a smaller cousin to the Pit, I figured it was a close enough match without being too suspicious." At my look of alarm, she continues. "I swear I didn't break in and go through their stuff while you were out of town—I'm bold, not stupid. We were in there when you were searching for a file, remember? That's when I noticed the pictures sitting among a few collected pieces on the shelves. They looked really old— black and white with a tannish hue."

My face relaxes. "Good, because frankly I don't know the full extent of her abilities. I'd hate to discount the chance she could possess some type of super-sniffer and would know someone not in the seethe was in their apartment."

"Nope, rest assured, I didn't do anything illegal. Despite what you think of me taking the form of a dog to get close to her, I do have some sense of self-preservation. If I didn't, I wouldn't have survived in Romeo's pack as long as I did— despite you thinking I was 'hiding' as a man. Some situations you just steer clear of, like nosing around someone's private things without an invite to do so, no matter how tempting it may be."

"I'm glad you've got a good head on your shoulders."

She arches an eyebrow. "Is this the same guy who barged in here a few minutes ago ready to rip me a new asshole?"

Regret seeps in, but I refuse to feel guilty. "Come on... don't hold it against me. I was scared and you didn't tell me what the hell you were doing or why."

"Uh-huh. God forbid your girlfriend has an idea of merit on her own?"

"Don't go putting words in my mouth, Candy." I smile, aiming for devilish and full of innuendo. "I'd much rather have something *else* in my mouth."

My hands trail down, whisper soft and full of promise, but not pushy in case she's still mad and not interested. A sigh escapes and tension leaves her body, as if she's melting into my touch.

Not hearing a no, I take things further, lowering her to the couch and proceeding to kiss my way from her ear down her neck. Another soft sound of acceptance spills forth, encouraging me further, and I bite down gently on the skin between her neck and shoulder, mimicking the traditional bite werewolves use to mark a mate. A shiver shudders through her, seeming to coax her back from the edge of sensual bliss.

"Oh, really?" she rasps in a teasing tone, as my fingers delve under the edge of her shirt. "What else could you want in your mouth... *my tongue?*"

I chuckle against her heated flesh, and nip her once more. God, I want so badly to bite through her flesh and mark her as mine. In time, I remind myself, in time.

Deciding on my next point of attack, I ease her shirt up, exposing her stomach and sheer bra. Drawing the stiff point of her nipple into my mouth, I suck the tip, gently biting down when her back arches in pleasure.

"Oh," she whispers, thrusting her hands through my hair and holding tightly. "I see you've found what your mouth wants."

A rumbling, deep hum bubbles from me, teasing and tantalizing her as the vibrations cascade from my mouth through every nook and cranny of her body.

She squirms and wiggles, apparently as motivated to feel my hot skin sliding against hers as I am. After a moment of rearranging herself, her hands fly to the top of her pants, eager to remove the obstacles between us.

"Get those off," I say in a rough voice, "and I'll show you exactly what I want in my mouth."

CHAPTER SEVEN: VIVIAN

"Good evening, Margery," I say upon entering the resort's walk-in refrigerator, my hands full with vials of my blood. "I didn't expect to see you here." With no guests on the resort, I figured the kitchen would be empty at this hour of the morning.

The resort doctor turns and smiles at me, tucking a loose strand of short, auburn hair behind an ear. "How else do you think the stores of frozen blood donations make it to the fridge for consumption?"

"Touché." I keep my face neutral. Dammit, I thought Rafe handled the freezing and defrosting of the blood supply. How much of what I think I know is right? Is my memory compromised in more ways than I'm aware? Shaking off the worries, I continue toward the shelf holding the bags marked for members of the seethe. No matter what, I've got to keep moving forward.

"Adding a little special something for the boys?" Margery asks while motioning to the vials as I set them down. "You're spiking their bags with the ancient blood we sell in the bar, right? I wondered how they were able to awaken while the sun was still up. But that makes sense."

"Yes, I am. It's the best way to rouse a sleeping vampire without putting them in a situation where they wake thinking they have to fight for their lives." I'm referring to the "love taps" Drew is not averse to delivering to a slumbering vampire who needs to rise before the sun sets. After hearing Paul retell his experiences, it sounds like Drew might enjoy that aspect a little too much.

"Ah, Drew's heavy-handed methods. I heard about a recent slap-fest from the chef."

I nod and busy myself with setting out the vials and needle.

If not for the spiking, and without Drew slapping them awake every night, they may not be able to resist the pull of the sun and rise at all during the summer months—which would leave them raving blood-lunatics by the time real darkness swung back around to our region.

Grabbing the marker from my pocket, I write Paul's name on seven of the bags. Next, I use the hypodermic needle and draw out five CCs of blood from the flat bottom vials. After repeatedly injecting my blood into each receptor at the top of the bag, I move to seven new bags, and inject only four CCs, marking them for Asa.

"Vivian, I've noticed our frozen blood stores have grown significantly in the past few weeks. Are you expecting trouble?"

I lift an eyebrow over her observations and raise my shoulders a tiny bit. "Not sure. But it doesn't hurt to be prepared." I wasn't the one who ordered more donations, so it must be something Asa initiated while we were away.

Worry clouds the lovely woman's face. "You neatly avoided my question about trouble." She smiles, a gentle curving of her mouth. "Should any of us be planning an extended trip off the resort for a while?"

Her question hits close to my heart. The hotel is less than one-third staffed during the summer, and technically, we don't even need most of them here. Eric mentioned the same thing at the debriefing, about possibly evacuating the resort. Maybe it's time to do so. "You bring up a very valid point. I have no idea what's in store for us, there's a lot of unknown brewing on the horizon. But just to be safe, maybe it would be best if we announced a one month mandatory vacation from the property. With full pay, of course."

My idea doesn't seem to inspire the relief I was hoping for, if anything, she appears more disturbed at the suggestion. "Oh. I see." One thing we don't need is any type of panicked energy leaking out to our human residents.

I step forward and stare deeply into the aging doctor's serene blue-green eyes. It takes less than a second to slip into her mind. "You're not going to be worried about the upcoming announcement for a required vacation. You'll remain neutral and not indulge publicly with speculation. You're going to visit family and travel, relaxed and content that nothing is happening at the resort while you're away."

I pull my will back, leaving her unaware I'm influencing her thoughts. "A visit with family sounds like a great idea!" the doctor says with joy in her tone. "My niece had a baby this past spring and I'd love to spend some time with them."

She turns away from me and resumes her task, which

appears to be checking freshness dates on the other blood bags. In another minute, I'm done and clearing up my supplies, organizing the bags with the oldest date on top before I leave.

The doctor finishes at the same time and we leave the fridge together. She hesitates by an old pencil sketch in the dining room, one of a Kodiak bear as it forages for food on a hillside. "Vivian, before I go, I've been meaning to ask you something. This drawing has been hanging here for years—I really like it. Where did you get it? The artist's style appeals to me. And if I'm not mistaken, I've seen a couple other prints, and watercolors, throughout the resort that look like they may have been done by the same hand."

The doctor's question catches me off-guard, a bloom of pleasure filling me. There's no harm in admitting what she wants to know, so I say, "Thank you for the kind words, and your interest. As a matter of fact, I drew it. And I'm also the one who created the others you've noticed throughout the property as well. Good rule of thumb with the artwork here—unless you see a signature somewhere on the front, it's probably mine."

Surprise flits across the doctors face, settling into a delighted smile. "I wondered if it could be you. But I wasn't sure. I'm glad I asked. You do beautiful work."

"Thank you. When you've lived as long as I have, it's good to take up new skills." A smile stretches my face, a feeling of closeness with the doctor that haven't felt before, flaring to life. "You know, Doctor, now that I have you here..."

"You mean now that you're actually talking to me?" Dr. Cook laughs. "I've always been here, Vivian. You're welcome to talk to me about anything that might interest you."

The smart woman stares boldly into my eyes, her

knowledge and interest of who and what I am blazing front and center—along with her unwavering trust. The few humans who know a vampire don't normally stare them in the eye. Dare I add "confidant" to her skill set? Would confiding in her be wise of me? Well, desperate times call for desperate measures. "Doc, I wanted to ask you about memories, the brain, and how we store knowledge. And inversely, how we hide known truths from ourselves."

"Hmm…. There is a reason there's an entire medical field devoted just to the brain. Neuroscience is not my specialty, but we obviously covered it in medical school. And I'm not so old that I've forgotten the basics, or haven't kept up with my continuing education. I'm happy to be of help. But memory is a tricky thing. Trauma, tragedy, grief, shame—lots of things we experience can alter memories. Is there something specific you wanted to know?"

"As you may have guessed, I've lived a very long life. So long in fact there are parts I don't remember." The doctor's eyebrows rise on her lightly furrowed forehead. I've got her attention now. "I was wondering if maybe, there's a way to perhaps recall things that I have worked hard to forget."

"Ah, that can be difficult. The lies we tell ourselves can quickly become the only truth we remember. Maybe 'forgetting' was used as a defensive trait if the experience was something very traumatic. Could that be the case here?"

"That's where it gets tricky, Doc. If I can't remember *why* I wanted to forget something, then I don't know what initially happened to make me want to forget it in the first place. Do you see what I mean?"

"Yes, I think so. I'm not sure what help I can be. One thing I can tell you—the strongest of our six senses to help with memory recall is scent. I don't know if that's a possibility for you, especially depending on how old the memories are we're talking about, as it could be even harder to track down coordinating scents.

"Looking at old pictures can help trigger memories, too. Or maybe visiting a place were a significant occurrence happened in your life, might bring back a memory. Oh, and you could always try hypnosis." My look must speak volumes, because she rushes on. "Don't discount it out of hand. It's just a thought. There's lots of tricks law enforcement officers use when interviewing a witness. They walk them through questions that touch on our senses, hoping to release details the witness couldn't remember initially."

Her suggestions intrigue me. While I can't immediately travel to another location to jar a memory into resurfacing, there's certainly one place to find an awful lot of old stuff. The storage rooms in the tunnels. And maybe if I'm lucky, there'll be a bunch of old smells associated with the stored items, too.

How much do I want to remember? Am I willing to open myself to the hurt that could be waiting for me?

I glance back at the sketch on the wall, one I did years ago while out exploring the tundra. If I can recall the time with my old turns, I could draw their likenesses. Could they be accurate enough depictions to help Asa with tracking down the people from my journals?

Definitely food for thought.

"Thank you, Margery. You've given me a great place to start."

The doctor looks pleased, and still a little surprised. I'm glad I asked for her advice.

"Well, then, I wish you good hunting," she winks, "memory hunting that is."

A truer choice of words was never spoken. I'll be hunting all right, but not necessarily for memories.

We say our farewells and the doctor leaves, a content expression on her face as she mumbles about the packing she's got to do. Her suggestions really got me thinking. And now I know exactly where to start: the tunnels.

God, I love this place. This vast and lavish resort is certainly not my first V V Inn, but it is the best one ever we've ever created. As I descend into the concrete tunnel, a sense of joy infuses me. There's nothing like the feeling of a perfectly designed escape route to reassure you that all is right in your world—and if it's not, to not worry because you have a backup plan that's fail-safe.

Sure, these tunnels were a bitch for the workers to build, and it took almost a decade, but the peace of mind their existence brings was worth it.

I step off the last rung of the ladder and close my eyes. Instantly, the energy within the tunnels fills me, and an internal map of the intricate passageways lights up in my mind. Every tunnel and door were designed to look exactly the same. I imagine a good blow to the head might mess up Asa or even Rafe when they travel down here, but thanks to my connection to every *thing* built on the property, I'll never have that issue.

Literally, I could be dropped anywhere in here blindfolded and I'd never be lost for a second. My internal compass would re-orient based on the blood, sweat, and tears from every worker who ever toiled on the resort and their blood bond through me, accessed via my extended consciousness.

Striding with confidence down the passage, I make my way toward an old weapons cache hidden in one of the seemingly "abandoned" storage rooms. Even the empty rooms hide something, you just have to know where to look. After six turns and three reinforced steel doors, I enter a dark room and flick on the overhead light. This room was never empty, and now the wooden crates have been pushed aside with some lids off. Hmm... what happened in here? I take a deep breath to see if I can sense any trace of who was here recently.

There. It's barely discernible. A subtle hint of death in the air. Very light. Like a brush against my senses, nothing more.

Ah, I remember now. This is the room that also houses one of my old sea chests filled with gold. Which means, this is where I instructed Asa and the reaper Lisa to search for gold doubloons a couple weeks ago. They needed them to pay the ferryman for the transportation of the inn's ghosts across the river Styx. Their dead souls were trapped here after recently meeting a grizzly end, and Asa and Lisa worked together to clean up our ethereal plane.

Deciding the open crates are as good as any place to trigger memories, I reach inside the closest one and dig through the contents. My hand touches smooth wood, and I draw out a medium-sized, ornate box. It appears to be made of mahogany and hand-carved with gold pieces inserted on the corners and embedded in some of the design work.

No doubt the box is a work of art on its own. So what could it hold inside? My first thoughts are colored with annoyance—why don't I recognize this damn thing? When did I get it? Who gave it to me? Did I steal it or buy it?

I don't like these unfamiliar feelings swirling through me, they make me doubt myself. And doubt is not what I need. I need to be strong. I need to be driven, and I need to protect those I love. How can I when I don't even remember who I am?

You know who you are. You're a killer.

I shake off the dark thought. I am more than a killer. And I have always been more than just a weapon. I will not allow the darkness inside me to make my insecurities larger-than-life. They are as small and insignificant now as they were five hundred years ago. Fears and doubts only have strength if I give them strength. And I will not.

Done with my inner pep-talk, I lift the lid, eager to see what's inside. Rich black fabric lines the interior, its softness and quality immediate upon inspection. Nestled in the black material is a pile of tiny silver circles linked one to another, forming a fine chain-mail mesh. Frayed and faded material lines the back of the metal.

I know what these are, even if I don't know where they came from. They're silver hoods. Meant to be worn by a vampire to block out the power of a manipulator vampire. I doubt these were a gift. More than likely I took them from an enemy.

Closing the lid, I set the box aside. I don't have need of these at the moment, but perhaps they should be brought upstairs and shared with the others as an extra layer of protection when we're gone. I rummage through the crate deeper, pulling out a heavy drawstring bag about the size of a toaster. It's made of soft, tan suede and weighted down by its dense contents. Metal would be my first guess. I slip open the drawstring closure, and reach inside, to draw its contents out.

My hand brushes cool metal as fiery pain assaults my fingers. I draw my hand back quickly, surprised I found another store of silver so soon, and so close to the last one. Perhaps this entire crate was loaded with items from a significant point in my life. I'm not sure.

Frustration spills through me as I realize none of this is helping. I open the mouth of the bag and dump the contents onto the top of the wooden box.

The light hits eight circlets of silver, finely wrought and delicate, reminiscence of an ornate head piece a noblewoman might wear for dressy occasions. In a flash, a memory comes to me, unbidden and in full color.

Laughter fills the moonlit air as the couples dance across the gleaming hardwood laid over the grassy field. Brightly colored ball gowns cascade to the makeshift floor, fabric swooshing on each turn of the dancers. The smell of fresh blood carries on a slight breeze, tickling my nose and stirring my cravings.

But the strong, cloying scent of the undead lies stronger, reminding me to not let down my guard. Shiny, ceremonial circlets of lined silver grace the ancients' foreheads, catching the light as they dance. They wear the headpieces in tribute to our distant past, and to symbolize what we left behind when we fled Atlantis and the tyranny of manipulators.

My senses tingle with awareness. Danger and death lie heavy in the air. They don't know it, but I am the wolf among sheep—as much as vampires can be called sheep—for I am the one they wear the ancient circlets to protect against.

With a shiver, I shake off the memory, thrusting the wooden box and the circlets on its lid back into the crate. Ugh.

Walking through memories from my time with the Tribunal is not what I'd hoped for. Perhaps coming back later would be better. Besides, I need to liberate my old weapons before we leave. Might be better to focus on that.

Unable to ignore the rest of the mess, I straighten the wooden boxes, adjust their contents, and replace the lids. In a few minutes, I'm done and move toward a far corner, the opposite side of the room from the concealed pirate chest.

Counting from the top, I stretch on my toes to press the fifth cinder block down, and then step back. After a brief pause for the gears and levers to do their job, a door-sized section of the wall slides in and to the left, revealing an organized, hanging display of my old fighting leathers and weapons.

I stare at the well-oiled clothing and blades, debating on what I want to take with us when we start tracking my turns. When I last wore these items, times were different. The council had briefly hired me as a mercenary rogue-hunter centuries after my twenty years of service.

To hunt rogues, I often stuck to the shadows to avoid being seen. A woman wearing these items in the nineteenth century would have caused quite a stir. Now, I have no doubt I could walk fully-garbed in battle gear down most any city street and wouldn't attract attention, besides receiving polite inquiries on where I purchased the cool items.

Idly, I wonder if everything still fits. A smile spreads across my face. It's not like I've gained weight over the centuries—one of the best perks of being a vampire. Then again, I'm sure if I could eat real food that might change. A liquid diet does have its advantages, and disadvantages, too.

Deciding to give it a go, for fun, I strip out of what I

consider to be my manual-labor working clothes, jeans and a tee shirt, and pull on the tight leather pants, steel reinforced corset-like top, and the reinforced leather jacket, too. The style cuts on the clothing may not be current, but the quality and craftsmanship is unsurpassed. I check all the secret sheaths built into the sleeves, pant legs, and across the jacket back. All the ticking is still sound and solid, assuring me I'll be able to load up my favorite blades with no problem.

Wishing for a mirror down in my secret hidey-hole, I take out my phone and reverse the camera, moving it up and down to examine the fit. Black leather encases my every curve. Yup. I look damn good.

Vanity restored, I return my attention to the blades on the wall. After testing the edge, the throwing knives are the first ones I load into the forearm and bicep sheaths. Next comes the longer, machete-like blade down my spine, and then the daggers and short swords on my thighs. With the full complement of weapons, I should be able to withstand a lengthy battle against many opponents—which is a significant change from the normal one-on-one type of hunting required as an enforcer.

The key to surviving for as a long as I have is adaptation. First, I killed for survival, because I had no choice, it was them or me. Then, when I became an enforcer for the tribunal, I killed out of duty. I couldn't allow the confirmed rogues to continue hunting humans and murdering at will. Doing so not only endangered innocents, it risked our exposure—because a crazy vampire is not good at hiding what they are.

Once my twenty-year term of service to the tribunal was up, I worked in earnest to accumulate massive amounts of wealth, understanding even back then that having enough cash, however it's carried, could mean the difference between life and death.

Money usually equates to power, especially within the Tribunal. Their recent financial problems, which left them weak to temptation and willing to accept our proposition to hunt a rogue for profit, could have been avoided if they'd learned to manage their money better. That entire establishment bleeds cash.

And now, now I kill only when I have no other choice. It may seem like I don't hesitate when I make the choice to end a life, but that's only because I know if I don't, the lives of those I care about will be in danger.

Satisfied with my explorations, I grab my work clothes and return to our suite. Today is going to be a busy day. We've lots to do before we go after my turns.

CHAPTER EIGHT: RAFE

I t's quarter past nine in the morning and I'm waiting outside the apartment building for the wizard to collect his spell ingredients. We completed a brief employee interview, making sure he knows not to say too much about what he's doing here, or to mention anything about teaching me magic. His official title will be security consultant.

He told me about his late-night visit with Diane and exploring the greenhouses. It sounds like he'll settle in okay, especially with her to help him replenish spell ingredients and such.

Justin emerges from the apartment building's entrance, a large duffle bag in one hand. I wave him over to the jeep before climbing back into the driver's side. In a moment, the passenger side opens and Justin joins me.

"Where we off to first, boss?" he asks, unknowingly addressing me exactly as his brother Asa does.

I hand him a topographical map of the property. "We'll be heading to the northwest corner where the windmills are. The plan is to walk the property line and set the wards as far apart as you deem effective."

Justin nods while studying the map. I start the jeep and drive. In a few minutes he says, "This place is way bigger than I expected. How many acres did you say you guys have?"

"Over ten thousand. Which comes to about fifteen square miles."

He whistles long and steady. "Holy shit, that's big. I think the entire town where my mom went to high school was only two square miles."

"Where was that?"

"New Jersey. Little town in Morris County called Butler."

I nod, understanding he's filling the silence with idle chit chat. Which is fine by me. I don't know the man very well and he's going to be responsible for training me in magic. Might be good if we got to know each other better. I haven't had a teacher, besides Vivian, in well over half a century.

I clear my throat, uncharacteristic nerves and anticipation over learning a new skill churning in my middle. "So, what exactly are we going to do today?"

"You said you wanted highly secure protection wards around the property, so I thought we'd begin our lessons at the same time. You can learn as we go. Although, who the hell is going to wander onto your land way up here is beyond me. We're literally in the middle of nowhere."

"Yes, that's true. We're very isolated up here." I refrain from telling him unexpected werewolf hunters already made their way onto our land earlier this summer. But then again, those intruders knew where to find us and came looking for our inn specifically. Hopefully, the magical barrier we're constructing will give us one more line of defense against anything like that occurring again. "You are aware of the threat against Vivian and what Rolando and Persephone are planning, right? It would be highly stupid of us to ignore our weaknesses. That's where you come in. With your help, our remote resort will become an even greater fortress to protect us."

"Yes, I know about their crazy bat shit. I never did trust Persephone when I worked there." He shivers. "She always gave me the creeps. I never knew if my personal talismans were enough against her abilities. And you're right about not ignoring security weaknesses. I still don't think they'd be able to attack you here, with or without my help. But hey, it's your dime."

"We'll have to physically place each ward and connect them to one another, linking them to create a kind of magical early-warning detection system."

I nod. "What's in the bag?"

"Spell ingredients, casting bowls, ritual items... basic magic stuff." He looks down at the map again. "Your property's perimeter is bigger than I thought, too. Bad news—I don't know if we'll be able to cover all of it today. Good news—at least I've got enough supplies on hand to complete the task."

"How far apart were your wards in the Tribunal's neighborhood?"

We travel down a paved road and turn onto a narrow gravel drive. "A couple of hundred yards. But there's no way in hell we want to do that here. Have you done the math on your property line?"

"Yeah, it's around sixteen miles."

"Hmm... Is all of it accessible by road?"

"No, it's not."

The young wizard looks out the window and sighs. "Great, just great. So we'll be hoofing it?"

I hold back a smile. He's been in the city for way too long. "That's why I told you to wear hiking boots."

We drive past the windmills, where the seethe staged Emiko's death last winter. Seems like a lifetime ago, and yet, it's only been six months.

At least the snow is finally gone. Instead of Spring, we have what I like to call Mud Season. Thankfully, by this time of the year, the worst of it is gone. We'll find out soon enough if it's rained recently.

I park the car and grab the satellite GPS, punching in the coordinates for the nearest access point to the edge of our land.

"This it?" Justin asks while peering through the windshield.

"Not quite." This time I do smile. "Let's go." I open my door and get out, hearing his door close a moment after mine.

I head into the trees, Justin trailing behind me with the duffle bag. The ground underfoot is firm, not swamped with water, much to my delight. We're not normally here in July, and I couldn't recall if we'd be on solid ground. Glad it's the latter.

Justin motions his chin toward the woods. "These skinny trees remind me of the scrub pines in south Jersey, in an area called the Pine Barrens. Can't miss them when you're at the Jersey Shore." He pauses as a thought occurs to him. "Did you guys burn the area at one time and this is re-growth? Nothing looks very big. All the trunks are on the thin side."

"Nope, not here. We did burn to clear for building the inn, but that was decades ago and nowhere near here. Regarding the trees, they don't get much past thirty feet due to the permafrost."

"Permafrost? What's that?"

"Couple of feet below the surface stays frozen all year round."

"No shit? That's pretty damn cold."

"Made building a bit of a bitch."

"I bet. Hey, that made me think of something. My grandfather was a contractor, how do the builders up here construct foundations for homes and such?"

"Most homes in Alaska don't have a deep foundation. They sit on concrete slabs or on above-ground foundations, like pilings."

"But on the plane, you mentioned the command center for hotel security is in the main building's basement. That's below ground, right? How did you build it?"

Justin doesn't know about the underground system of tunnels, and I'm not sure if he will need to. He's only going to be here for a year and shouldn't need access to the master escape system my wife and I designed. "Same way the Army Corp of Engineers built the underground systems up in Barrow: fire, explosives, heavy machinery, and lots of patience."

"Fascinating. All the homes I knew of in Jersey had basements—well, except for the ones in flood zones. And in Argentina, it seemed hit or miss whether or not a place would have a basement. But most didn't."

"Will the existence of permafrost alter what you plan on doing today?"

"Thankfully, no. We'll be activating the ingredients at each location, then sprinkling them in the soil and on plant life. In essence, your entire resort will be linked through the earth and what lives on it, even in the frozen depths of winter."

I think about all the concrete, brick, and asphalt in the Tribunal neighborhood. Throughout the city there were only green spaces in parks, private buildings with inner courtyard gardens, and occasionally the rare patch of green, like his old yard, out behind homes. "Is this the same type of approach you used for the ancients?"

Justin shakes his head. "Nope. I had to place already-linked talismans at regular intervals and activate them with magic once they were in place. Since the property here is so vast, and much more organic than what we'd find in a city, we're taking a different approach. The plan is to bind each location to one another in a chain as the ingredients are scattered. Creating a kind-of magical force field, if you get my drift."

"Yeah, I think I understand. I'm curious to see how it all works."

"I'll have you watch the first two times, and then you'll take over the beginning steps at the third location."

"Okay."

We travel the rest of the way in silence, with me glancing at my GPS every so often and altering our course as needed. In ten minutes we reach the edge of the property line. This section of the resort contains lots of trees, all close to the same diameter in thickness. Justin comments on their size, and I explain how we don't get really tall, thick trees up here due to the aforementioned permafrost, since their root systems have to stay near the surface.

Justin sets his duffle on the ground and opens it. He removes several fabric bags and a dark purple cloth decorated heavily with embroidered symbols done in gold thread. Meticulously, he unfolds the material, spreads it on the ground and places a copper bowl in the center.

I watch as he adds measured ingredients from each bag, chanting a different phrase with each one he pours in. A part of me wonders if I should be taking notes and now I'm annoyed he didn't mention to bring a notebook or something. At least the phrases he's chanting are in English.

I wait until he's quiet to ask, "What's the distance we'll be placing these around the perimeter?"

Justin shoots me a dark look, glancing sharply at the spell bowl.

A light flush heats my cheeks. That's one way to find out I shouldn't be talking. Would have been nice if he'd told me in the beginning to be quiet.

The wizard reaches into his pocket and pulls out a glass vial filled with a red liquid. The bottle stopper looks to be a rubberized dropper, and my guess is confirmed when he unscrews it, pinches the top, and then draws out a thin glass tube filled with liquid. I'm assuming it's blood, but I won't know for sure until I can ask.

He dispenses two drops into the bowl while repeating "Like binds to like, bring forth protection against all who mean harm" as each drop falls. On the last one, a poof of air, like a wind, pushes against me, its origin appearing to come from the direction of the bowl.

"Wicked," I say, before I can stop myself. Hey, this stuff is freaking cool. Feels like I'm living a real-life Harry Potter movie and I have to hold back my desire to grunt like Hagrid.

This time I don't get the dark look, just a small lopsided grin from the wizard to indicate he's heard me.

"Next, we burn the bowl's contents and scatter the ashes," Justin says. He withdraws a lighter from his back pocket and grabs a thin piece of wood from his bag.

"Don't you have a spell for fire?"

"Yes, but with the amount of work we plan on doing today, I'd rather not exhaust myself. The lighter is a smarter use of limited resources. And to answer your earlier question, we'll be placing these every half mile. If the boundary feels weak, we'll come back and place new links at the quarter-mile interval."

"Geez, that's an initial thirty-two locations we'll have to set."

Justin nods. "Like I said before, I don't expect us to get it all done in one day."

I glance at my watch. "It's early, and we have almost nonstop daylight this time of year. Depending on how often we take breaks, we may be able to do it."

The wizard picks up the bowl and drops in the lit piece of wood. He repeats the binding phrase again, over and over, while the ingredients steadily burn. Once the fire burns itself out, he uses the heel of his hiking boot to create a long furrow in the soil, and scatters the ashes in.

Justin waits until he's covered up the ashes before responding, "I was more concerned over the time it would take to travel to each location. It might be worth it to walk along the boundary line from here, rather than to go back to the jeep and drive, and then walk out to the line again."

"Good point," I say while mentally calculating how long it will take us to walk and preform the ritual at each half-mile point. Depending on the tundra and frost upheavals, he's right, this task could take longer than one day. "Should I have been taking notes on the phrases and steps you did?"

"No." He digs in his pocket and hands me a folded sheet of paper. "This will make it easier. You'll need to memorize each step and phrase."

I nod, grateful for the help, and open the page. The steps are neatly mapped out, all the ingredients, in order, with the phrases recorded, too.

Justin carefully repacks all the supplies, tightens each ingredient bag, and folds his ceremonial cloth with precise movements. I watch like a hawk, eager to not make a mistake when it's finally my turn to try.

"Whose blood did you use?" I ask.

"I used Vivian's. Figured it made the most sense over using my own since it's your property."

"Good call. I'll make sure your supply is replenished. That's the payment she gave you in Buenos Aires, right?"

"Yeah, and I'd wanted to use it sparingly, so I appreciate the refill."

"No problem. Consider it a job perk." A part of me is curious how much of my own blood it would take to activate and fuel the warding spell, but Justin has a good plan in place with Vivian's blood and I see no need to muck it up by cutting myself at every half-mile mark. Even if I would like to see the results.

Maybe we could use my blood for the quarter mile points in-between. That might be a good way to bind the ward to both of us.

I take out the GPS unit again and grab my cell phone to call the command center. Better to let them know our progress and keep them updated of our location.

CHAPTER NINE: JON

I t's a late morning when I slip from the cabin, leaving my slumbering girlfriend tucked in bed. With the amount of daylight we have right now, time is kind of relative, especially when you've been up all night, and most of the morning, making love.

The quiet of the property wraps me in silence, welcoming me to the secluded peace I always find in the woods. I need to practice and perfect the ability to half-shift, and even though Candy might be a great person to ask because of her mad shifting-skills, I'd prefer to at least make an attempt on my own.

Don't get me wrong, I'm glad we cleared the air, but I'm still not thrilled at the position she's put me in with Vivian and Rafe. Not telling them about her and our relationship is clearly a lie by omission. And I know I'll have to come clean eventually. It's the when, where, and how that's giving me the most stress. Not to mention being worried about Vivian's reaction. Will she freak out? How would any master vampire react to their servant being with someone else intimately? Would it make a difference if the relationship was serious or casual?

Which leads me to the inevitable, is Candy *the one?* Is she my mate? Would I have felt attraction for Magda if my destiny was with Candy?

Physical attraction to another person does not mean Candy isn't right for you. Chemistry is just that, chemistry. N*ot acting on every impulse you experience is called maturity and restraint.*

The inner wisdom and my many options roll over in my mind while I venture deeper into the woods, pushing my worries with Candy to the back so I can focus on what needs to be done. With Magda, I practiced the half-shift indoors. And later, when I practiced with Viv and Rafe nearby, we were also inside.

Maybe the key to mastering this ability is connecting with my wolf in a natural setting—at least until I know what the hell I'm doing. Magda showed no problems half-shifting wherever she was, whenever she wanted. Just like any skill, I'm sure that kind of mastery must come only with lots of practice.

Before I can decide exactly where to go, I look up to discover I've wandered to the clearing where Ivan killed one of my wolf-dogs last winter. Spindly plants have grown and the snow no longer remains, but the images and feelings from that night come screaming back to the forefront of my mind.

The animal's bloodied, lifeless form laid frozen to the ground. The crippling rage and grief seizing me that day were paralyzing. Rafe, Vivian, and Asa were there as well, and each helped in their own way. God, it was awful.

As the remembered misery of the moment flows over me, I experience the sensation of an epiphany. My dog's death *is* the reason to do this—to protect every living thing relying on me for safety, not just the humans and my small pack of werewolves. My skills, my very essence as a werewolf, needs to evolve to the next level. I never want to experience that type of crippling anguish ever again.

A nudge to my left thigh brings my attention downward. One of my dogs, Kujo, leans heavily against my leg, staring straight ahead into the woods. I run a hand through the soft fur between his ears, allowing the peace from the animal's company to fill me. In less than a minute, we're joined at the clearing by a dozen other dogs, all of them calm and relaxed.

They're free from their kennels to roam the property during the daylight hours. It's only in the winter I worry about their overexposure to the extreme climate conditions. Why are they here now? Are they more mentally connected to me than I give them credit for? Could they have sensed my conflicted thoughts and came to lend their physical presence in support?

My body fills with a lightness I can't explain. As if the weight of the world has been removed from my shoulders and I can accomplish anything. A true alpha draws on the strength of his pack, and why it never occurred to me that these dogs are just as able to offer their energy as the werewolves, I'm not sure.

Whatever the reason for them being here, I'll not question it. I'm grateful for each and every furry body in my circle who depends on me—hell, in reality, I depend on them, too. Their friendship and unconditional love would warm the hardest heart.

Eventually, all the animals settle to the ground, and so do I, sitting on the spongey soil with my legs crossed under me. Drawing on the techniques and visualization suggestions Magda taught me a few days ago, I reach for the magic within to trigger the transition from man to wolf.

Slowing the transformation process is my biggest challenge. Normally, my full shift occurs in a matter of seconds, so finding the internal balance to ease into a half-shift is extremely tricky.

My first dozen tries are unsuccessful, where I shift straight to a wolf while still fully clothed. Each time, I resist the compulsion to wiggle out of the clothes to free my transformed limbs and run. Instead, I return to human form. After I transition back multiple times, my muscles show signs of strain, shaking slightly from the effort of reshaping over and over again.

As air wheezes in and out of my lungs, I ease back to lie on the ground, struggling momentarily to get an arm back through a shirtsleeve. Only once did I complete any type of partial shift, and it was my hand. I'm going to need a lot more time to get this skill perfected. I stare up through the tree branches at the cloudless blue sky, willing myself to breathe deeply.

The closeness of the pack feels soothing and supportive. A dog to my left stirs, standing to sniff the air. He releases a soft whine and a few moments later Candy steps out of the woods.

"I wondered where you were. You've been out here for a while. Still mad at me?" she says, with a grin on her face.

She knows I'm not mad. There's no way we could have made love for hours and then I walked away mad at her. That kind of emotional connection and intimacy wipes out the anger and frustration like a one-two punch combination.

"Nah, you know I'm not." I return her smile. "Although, I

still feel a twinge of annoyance. You really have put me in a bind with Vivian."

"Okay, then. Let's tell her."

I cough, my heart clutching in my chest at the suggestion. Maybe she didn't mean what I thought she meant. "What?"

"You know," she says, wiggling her eyebrows. "Let's tell her about *us*. Let me meet her for real. You guys are going to be leaving soon and I don't want any lingering tension between the two of you, or between us."

"Really? You mean it? What about wanting to get to know her and all that bull?"

Her eyebrows draw together, creating a crease in her smooth forehead. "It's not bull and you know it. Besides, I have met her. I did get a feel for her. And I also think you're right. If we drag this charade out much longer, it's liable to backfire on us."

"So, just like that, eh?" I reach for her hand and pull her down next to me on the ground. "You're ready to commit to you and me?" I hear the hopeful note in my voice and wish it wasn't there. It's hard to hide what I really want: a mate and a partner. Despite popular dating trends, I'm not so sure hiding what I feel from someone I'm falling for is the best course of action.

There's no guarantees in life. Hell, Vivian is a good example of that. From the bits and pieces I've picked up over the years, I know she's had *at least* two husbands before Rafe. And when you consider how many people she willed herself to forget, she could have had many, many more even she isn't aware of.

"Yes, I'm ready," Candy says, a wistfulness in her expression. "I'm willing to commit to the here and now and see where we go. I hold no illusions going in. If things don't work out between you and me, *or* between the two of them and me, I'm pretty sure Vivian would wipe my mind of anything she didn't want me to know."

"Yeah. That's probably exactly what would happen. But I'm just guessing."

My girlfriend glances at me with a touch of incredulity in her eyes. "How do you know she hasn't done the same thing to you over the years?"

I sit up a little straighter. "What do you mean?"

"You know, like if you acted against her wishes, or learned something you shouldn't have. How do you know she hasn't removed the memories or knowledge from your mind?"

I shrug. "If you want to get technical, you're right, I don't know for sure. How the hell could I? But I trust her. She made a promise to me years ago when we first arrived here, when I was still learning more about her and the inn. She assured me she would never steal from my mind. Never erase anything or force me to do something I didn't want to."

"And you trust she's never done it?"

"That's what being in a relationship means. Even a mostly platonic one, like ours. You have to trust the other person with parts of yourself that are vulnerable. Have faith they won't abuse your conviction. And bottom line, I trust Viv and Rafe with my life."

Candy nods, like she already guessed as much. "I understand. It makes sense. And logically, it's the only way you can be with a vampire. Either you trust them, or you don't."

"So where do you stand? It seems pretty early for you to be making a decision this large."

"I trust you, and you trust them. That's good enough for me."

I squeeze her hand while a light breeze ruffles the branches overhead. Aside from the mosquitos, otherwise jokingly called Alaska's state bird, the inn and grounds are gorgeous in the summer, making it joy to be here.

"Now that that's settled, what are you doing out here with all the dogs?"

"Remember that half-shift skill I learned from Magdalena?" She nods. "I've only been able to force my hand to half-change, but it doesn't last long."

"Do you want help from me?"

Surprise colors my response. "Why do you think you'd have to ask? I'm struggling to figure this shit out. And after a couple of hours of trying, I'm grateful for anything you'd care to share."

A shy upturn of her lips appears on her radiant face. "Really?" At my nod, her smile grows. "Okay then. I wasn't sure if my input would be welcome or if you'd be annoyed."

"No ego here, babe. I'm clueless on how to harness this and after dozens of attempts, my brain—and body—feels like mush."

"All right. Glad to hear it. You'll be open to trying what I suggest if you've already exhausted other techniques. When I change into a new animal I've never tried before, I usually have to put more effort into it. But it's not like it's mentally or physically difficult, just that it requires more concentration."

I nod to encourage her to keep going—the faster I learn this, the more help I'll be to Vivian and Rafe when we leave to track down her turns.

"When you shift to a wolf," she asks, "do you have to

picture becoming a wolf in your mind?"

"No. It happens so fast there's almost no thought or effort on my part. I'd call it almost instantaneous if that was possible."

She nods, as if remembering my changes in her mind. "Instead of trying to halt your change mid-shift, have you tried visualization techniques of certain body parts? Like, stare at your hand and picture it exactly how you want it to look in this 'half-form' you're aiming for."

I stretch my neck from side to side, attempting to relax and ease my aching muscles. "If you think it'll work, I'll give it a try. How do I start?"

"Here," she says, a gentle hand on my shoulder pushing me to lay back down on the ground. "Close your eyes for a moment." I do as she says. "Picture the changed hand in your mind. Every detail."

"Okay. Doing that."

"Now tell me what you see."

"My hand is over twice its normal size, reddish brown fur covers the back, with thick-knuckled fingers tipped in long, razor sharp claws, curling inward slightly at the ends."

"Good," she says, her voice softer and lower than before. "Now reach for the magic within your blood, not with your full attention, but rather like you're taking an absent-minded sip of a very hot drink."

My brows scrunch together in confusion, not quite liking her analogy of the drink, but I try nonetheless.

"Do you feel the spark within you, Jon?"

"It's more of a raging fire, but I think I've got the gist of it."

"Open your eyes and raise your arm 'til you can see your hand."

I follow her directions, staring at my hand—which still looks like a hand, so far.

"Picture what you just described, Jon. Imagine your hand is exactly like you told me. Long, knobby fingers with ragged claws. Powerful hands strong enough to bend a rebar in half."

I smile at her embellishments, but do as she instructs.

"Call that spark within you, press it toward your arm."

Not quite sure of what she expects at this point, I try and picture a spark from that raging fire, and that I'd like it to go to my hand.

"Don't give up, Jon. I can feel the magic inside you. It's white hot and powerful."

I overlay the desired hand image in my mind again and fur begins to sprout from my skin.

"You're doing it, babe! I see hair growing."

Next, my skin expands, feeling tight, almost like it's swelling instantly from an injury or excessive fluids. And then the nails lengthen, sprouting from my fingertips like a special effect from a movie gone horribly wrong.

"Holy shit, I'm doing it."

"Yes! I knew you could."

My large werewolf hand looks odd attached to my regular arm, but I don't care. I'm thrilled with the progress so far. "More. I need to do more."

"Picture the change on your other hand, Jon. Let's walk through this one body part at a time." Her tone changes when she catches sight of my shaking hand. "How do you feel, are you tried or can you keep going?"

"Considering this is the best I've done all morning, you're damn right we're going to keep going." I've got to master this skill. Before it's too late.

CHAPTER TEN: ERIC

Alaska.

Its vast and glorious expanse spreads below the flying propeller plane. For our flight down to Fairbanks, Pat's piloting under Drew's watchful eye, and I don't mind relaxing and enjoying the view one little bit.

If someone had told me years ago I'd wind up living here, I'd have laughed. Our dad was in the Air Force decades ago and we were stationed here for a short period of time—but my brothers and I were pre-school age and don't remember any of it. Most of the old pictures from that time frame didn't survive our numerous moves. But I'd always wanted to visit as an adult and see what the place was like.

Traveling from location to location with military parents seemed adventurous as a kid, but I often wondered if it was the military that ruined my parents' marriage, or was it their unhappiness with each other, and their lives, that did it? Would we all still be together if my dad had stayed in past his last term?

I shake my head in the negative. I doubt it. It's not easy to admit, but they were unhappy no matter where we lived, or who Brett worked for. Divorce was better all around. Although, I never forgave our mother for taking Justin and leaving. We always suspected she had a favorite out of the three of us, and that it was Justin, but having it proven by her actions really sucked.

Holidays just weren't the same after they left. Not depressing or anything, more like we felt their missed presence at the dinner table and around the tree. But seeing our dad happy the rest of the time was worth it.

Whether my mom and Justin were in our lives or not, Asa and I probably would have joined the military anyway, as neither one of us had any clue what to "do" with our lives. Going to college without direction would have been a waste of time and money—money we didn't have. And the idea of accumulating student loans when I didn't know what I wanted to do seemed like a dumb idea.

Despite the sand pit of hell we were sent to fight in, being in the military wasn't so bad. I learned a lot. Met people I'll probably never see again. And I grew up. A smile creases my face as I recall being on leave and partying with Pat in the woods last fall back in West Milford.

The real mistake came when we tried to drunkenly *save* a mangy dog wandering the woods—we thought we'd get it back to its owners. Turned out not to be a lost dog, but a crazed werewolf intent on killing anything it encountered.

Later, we learned the attacking werewolf was visiting the area while on vacation with the rest of Romeo and Elsa's pack. After we recovered from our injuries and understood what we'd become, Pat and I lived with Jon's old alpha, up in Canada, for several months.

I run a finger over the wolf charm dangling from the paracord bracelet around my wrist, its camouflage coloring reminding me of my time in the Army. Elsa's teenage nephew Jack made the bracelets for everyone in the Manitoba pack, and I'm glad I kept mine after we left. It's a nice keepsake of the time I spent there. Living with a large and boisterous group like theirs had good points and bad points, that's for sure.

Rampaging teenage hormones have *nothing* on a werewolf trying to find their mate. It was like a hedonistic horn-fest. I understand why Jon wanted to leave. It could be a bit much, even if you were okay with exchanging partners often. Although, I'm not really speaking from personal experience. Pat and I were shot down by the stuck-up bitches nine times out of ten. No one wanted a "puppy," as they loved to call us.

While I might not have chosen this fate for myself, it sure as hell beats the alternative—which would have been dying in the forest that night from our extensive wounds.

I shake myself out of the old thoughts and keep my attention focused on the view. The next few hours fly by uneventfully, just like every other time. We land, visit the post office, collect what's going to the resort, and load the large truck. After an early lunch at the closest restaurant, Pat and I return to the airstrip.

The gravel drive leading to the hangar lies bumpy and littered with potholes. Cursing, Pat swerves around the obstacles. I don't know why, but I expected better of Fairbanks. Maybe because it's the closest thing to a real city up here. But the road conditions are par for the course with being out in the middle of nowhere. I don't know how bush pilots land in "empty" fields, and I'm not looking forward to the landing lessons where Drew will force me to learn, either.

Pat parks the truck next to the plane and we unload the bins of mail to the hold. Looks like Diane has been shopping online again, she sure has a ton of boxes addressed to her with the Amazon smile on them. Flying down weekly is much easier now in the constant daylight, that's for damn sure. I'm not looking forward to night landings and instrument flying, which we'll be doing once the season change occurs.

Pat signals the all clear as far as packages, and parks the vehicle behind the hangar Viv and Rafe own. After checking the plane over, we climb inside, where Drew has been holed up since we landed.

"Took you guys long enough," he says from the shaded back seat, where he's covered head to toe in light-blocking fabric. It looks like he's wearing a wet suit, truth be told, but what exactly the material is I have no idea. "And I smell cooked beef."

"Keep your panties on, fanghead," Pat says while climbing in. "Werewolves gotta eat, man."

I smile, buckling myself in. "Yeah, and Diane did a ton of online buying again. Not our fault."

"Yeah, yeah, whatever. Let's get going. It'll take us hours to fly back."

"What's the rush, old man?" Pat asks. "Got a hot date?" he wiggles his eyebrows suggestively.

I shake my head and begin the interior pre-flight check. Even though we landed recently, I know if I skip anything Drew will make me go back and start from the beginning anyway. Once I'm sure I've done everything, we're ready to roll. "All done. Okay if I get this tin can in the air?"

"Don't forget, radio your intentions to the main hangar and then contact our destination. You'll be all set."

"Check," I say and make the requested calls. After both are done, I start the engine and the propeller begins to whir. One last look down the runway to ensure no other planes are coming or going, and I pull into position. I've only been flying for a few months, but no matter what, I always feel a thrill when we taxi down the runway.

I slide the throttle in, and away we go, speeding down the asphalt to take flight. The wheels eventually lift and we're off, angling upward above the approaching tree line.

"Woohoo!" Pat yells from the co-pilot seat. "That shit never gets old."

He joined the Air Force when I joined the Army years ago, but he wasn't a pilot. And if you're not a pilot in the Air Force, you're pretty much a grunt—or at least that's how they make you feel.

I look over at my best friend. "Did you ever want to be a pilot, Pat?"

"Not back when I first joined. And then after I was in a while and got to know some of the cocky sonsabitches who were pilots—the answer was still nope. I had no desire to learn. Goddamn, they were some arrogant fuckers. Like the sun rose and set from their ass."

Drew laughs from the backseat. "You must not feel that way now. Look at you. You almost have as many hours as Eric —and you're well on your way to having your license."

"Thanks in large part to you," Pat motions with his head toward Drew, "and that freaky-ass wetsuit that makes you look like you're a lost undersea explorer."

"Would you rather have waited until the darkness to learn?"

"No, thanks. I'm good." He kicks back and lazily looks out the window. "If the view wasn't so gorgeous up here this would totally suck."

We continue on an uneventful flight for the twenty minutes, until a red light appears on the dash.

"Uh-oh," Pat says. "What did you do, dude? I don't know what that light means."

Before I can read the tiny print under the gauge, Drew answers from the back. "It's the fuel gauge. I'll ignore your comment that you didn't know what it was, you slacker."

"That can't be right," I reply. "I filled it when we landed."

"Yeah, I heard you do it." The vamp shrugs. "Could be a malfunction with the gauge. We can check it when we land."

Ten minutes later another light goes on. This time it's for the engine. "Uh, Drew. Should we be worried?"

Drew leans forward, examining the lights on the control board. "Huh. That is odd." He reaches an arm between the seats and thumps his fist above the dials. "Not sure what's going on."

"And banging on the control panel is a good idea?" Pat asks, a slight tremor of fear in his voice. "I'm not liking this, guys..."

While Drew and I waste precious seconds looking for a possible cause, the engine seizes and the propeller stops moving.

"Oh shit!" Pat screams. "Turn it back on, dude." He motions toward the wheel. "Fucking do something!"

I fumble for the ignition, hoping it's just stalled, like a car. I turn the key back to the start position and frantically grind it forward, hoping that will help.

"Grab the wheel, Eric," Drew commands. "Hold the plane steady. Stay calm. We're not going to drop out of the sky. Move, man," he says to Pat, tugging on his shoulder. "Let me up here."

His calm, assured voice reduces the racing of my heart. I'm trying my best not to freak out and piss myself, but my mind draws an utter blank on what to do next. All I can think of is to try and recall the stuff we covered about emergency landings. And absolutely nothing comes to mind. It's like my brain blanked on everything I learned.

Pat scrambles to the back, and the tightness is my chest eases when Drew takes his seat. He buckles in and flips a few switches. Nothing happens. He grabs the wheel and the breath I was holding eases out.

"Brace yourselves, boys."

"What?" Pat asks, terror tinging his words.

"Nothing is working. The whole panel is dead. We've got no way to fix it mid-air. We're going to have to land."

The deep blanket of trees spreads out below us, offering no place to safely do as he's suggested. "Holy shit," I say, the enormity of our situation hitting me between the eyes like a thrown brick. "This can't be good."

"Not to worry," Drew assures us in an even voice. "We're all very hard to kill. We'll make it. It's the plane I'm worried about."

"Broken bones still hurt," Pat quips, unperturbed by Drew's calm acceptance. "And we can all die, and very quickly I might add, if this thing explodes in flames."

Drew maneuvers us as the plane slowly loses altitude.

"Can one of you check the map and see if there's a clearing or a river bed coming up? Something better than a forest of trees would be nice."

I grab the map and unfold it, ignoring the shaking in my hands.

"Come on, man," Drew says through gritted teeth. "We're losing altitude quicker now. Must have a tail wind driving us down."

I scan the dials in front of me, and then return my focus to the map, trying to determine where we are and what's nearby. "Uh...up ahead, to the right, over that ridge, there should be a stream."

"Thank-fucking-God we haven't had any rain recently," Pat mumbles while clasping his seatbelt in a death grip.

Drew angles the plane to the right, and as we pass a low hill the dry creek bed comes into view. "Crap, that's gonna be a tight squeeze."

The small plane dips down, gliding slowly closer to the fast-approaching ground, its wings held steady by Drew's strength and sheer determination.

"We're going to die!" Pat screams, his voice pitching higher with anxiety and distress, as he covers his eyes to avoid seeing what's ahead.

"Not...if...I...can..." Drew grits his teeth while forcing the answer out slowly, "help it!"

The oncoming scenery appears crystal clear, as if my werewolf eyesight doesn't want me to miss one small detail of our swiftly-arriving landing.

"What can I do to help?" I ask, keenly aware I'm sitting here next to Drew doing nothing.

"Grab your wheel, too. The more hands the better at this

point. We're going to angle toward that dry bed down there. Do you see it?"

I look beyond the windshield once again, searching the trees for where he means. Up ahead the greenery parts, revealing gentle sloping sides down to a narrow stream bed. It looks way too small to land there. "Uh... yeah. I see it. I don't think the plane will fit."

"Won't fit?!?" Pat squeaks, prying his hands away from his eyes to peer forward and look for himself. "We're gonna die!"

"Jesus, Pat! Shut up!" I yell back. "How is that helpful?"

"Helpful? How the fuck do you think I can help? It's not like I have a fucking engine in my back pocket for crying out loud."

"Shut up, both of you," Drew says, his concentration focused ahead, on the slim area where the trees aren't growing.

He takes one hand away from the wheel and flips a couple of switches again, for what reason, I don't know. The plane is eerily quiet as we glide closer to the quickly-approaching ground. People survive plane landings like this all the time in Alaska. I'm sure we'll be fine.

Maybe if I keep telling myself that over and over it will come true.

The whir of the landing gear descending sounds underneath the plane. "Prepare yourselves," he says. "As in, hold on! We're going to touch down in a few seconds."

I grip the wheel hard, my arms locked at my sides. A slight brush of pressure below our feet indicates the tires have touched ground. Before I can release a sigh of happiness, the entire plane shifts, the view beyond the windshield becomes ground, and then sky again as the plane rolls forward and crashes, a wing ripping off, and the sound of screaming metal fills the air around us.

The seat belts hold us strapped to the seats as the windshield breaks and a whoosh of air comes in, followed by debris slamming around the cabin. I hear a scream of pain and then all goes black.

CHAPTER ELEVEN: VIVIAN

Dressed in body-hugging running pants and a trim tee shirt, I finish my stretching well before Rafe is scheduled to arrive for our sparring session. Expelling the amped up tension we've been dealing with is crucial to remaining focused on our goals—or so my loving husband insists.

I find my best tension-relievers usually involve him and I being naked, but that certainly won't happen when we've got an audience in the dojo. In times of conflict like this, when I worry I can't protect my loved ones, the darkness inside threatens to spill up and out, tempting me with the easy path of killing, instead of solving, my problems. Hence, why Rafe suggested we spar.

Breathe in.

Breathe out.

One moment at a time. That's what life is. A series of connected moments. Moments we can allow to overtake us, or moments we prepare for, accept, and withstand.

Air whooshes in and out of my lungs in a steady stream. Gradually, the worst of the anxiety fades and I'm left feeling only moderately stressed and ready to maim.

I can do this. I can master the worries and doubts plaguing me about this upcoming threat. I must stop Rolando and Persephone in order to keep my people safe. There is no other choice. I can no longer sit in my secluded fortress, content to watch the world from a safe distance.

Whether I like it or not, I must prepare to go forth and meet the threats awaiting us. Not allow those threats to come to our home.

I'm more than just a weapon. I am a vehicle for change.

Rafe better not try anything cute with me today, like his usual sexual teasing as distraction. He's done it in the past, to our mutual satisfaction, but I arrived early today for our session on purpose—with the intention to observe Asa and Paul, who are scheduled to be here the same time as us.

With that goal in mind, I move to a corner and stand still. Breathing shallowly, I meditate while Asa enters the training room and warms up. Standing in the shadows and being quiet can be advantageous. Especially if you want to track the training of your seethe without them getting nervous you're watching. I weave a simple illusion around myself, ensuring the casual observer would miss me at first glance. Outright invisibility isn't my objective, remaining unnoticed is.

Steps sound in the distant hallway, prompting Asa to check the wall clock while moving to the doorway. "Paul!" Asa calls. "You're right on time. Let's get started."

Paul follows him into the dojo, crossing the threshold and toeing off his shoes. "What are we working on today?" he asks, not sounding nearly as enthusiastic about his training as I'd hoped. Although, considering he's working with a highly-trained soldier, his reluctance could stem from fear. The other man is not only bigger and stronger, he also knows a lot more about fighting, which has been known to draw out Paul's insecurities in the past.

"Weapons or hands?" Asa asks, in an uncharacteristic show of understanding the chef's hesitancy.

Paul opts for hand to hand. They move into the center of the training mats to face off.

"Let's work on some defensive throws." Asa steps closer and puts his hands on Paul's arms. "Watch where I place my hands and feel how I grasp. You'll repeat the grip next."

He executes a series of moves designed to incapacitate his opponent and keep him on the floor. Then he has Paul run through the same actions again and again, while allowing himself to be used as the practice dummy.

"Muscle memory is key in a fight," Asa instructs, while subtly altering Paul's grip for better leverage. "You do a defensive move enough times and eventually you don't have to think about it, your body just moves."

Without trying, I'm able to read the self-doubting thoughts projecting loud and clear from Paul.

He's been saying the same type of positive bullshit with me for weeks now, but honestly, it feels like I'll never be as good as them.

I debate on responding, deciding to go with my gut. *If you think that,* I whisper softly into his mind, *then it's already true.*

Paul whips toward me, accurately pinpointing my location due to our mental connection. No longer needing the illusion, I drop it completely.

Asa sees his pupil's attention drift and turns toward me, too. "Care to join us?" he says with a smile. "There's plenty of room in here."

"That's why I came. Rafe wants to practice Krav Magra with me."

"Like in the Liam Nelson movies?" Paul asks. "Why am I not surprised?"

"You'll see, Paul. When you live a long time and travel as much as I have, you'll get a chance to learn a *lot* of things you never dreamed existed. Fighting styles being one of them. Every country has a deadly style and skills you can add to your repertoire, all you have to do is immerse yourself in the culture to discover it."

He returns his attention to Asa, but his mind still projects. *She makes it sound so freakin' easy, like you're traveling and sampling new foods, discovering recipes and combinations you've never thought of before. But maybe that's my cook's mind finding a correlation. If you were always training to survive and live another day, then perhaps noticing and assimilating the local fighting techniques would be the equivalent. I'm not sure.*

I decide not to let him know I've overheard him, and make a mental note to help him train his telepathic walls to be stronger.

Facing off the larger man, Paul raises his fists and widens his stance, a smirk on his face. "Dammit, Jim. I'm a cook, not a fighter."

I smile at his Star Trek reference, while Asa looks at him like he might have been hit too hard or something. Paul shrugs his shoulders and motions to the mat. "Are we done yet?"

Asa makes a show of glancing significantly at the clock. "Uh, noooo... We've been here fewer than twenty minutes."

"That's it?" Paul responds with a smile. "It seems so much longer."

Rafe saunters in, wearing clothes similar to mine. Tight and slick, leaving nothing to the imagination regarding the range and breath of his musculature. He weighs close to two hundred and thirty pounds. And at six foot two or so, that's pretty darn solid.

"Interesting outfit, Rafe," Asa says, eyebrows creeping up his head in surprise.

Rafe snorts and shakes his head. "Make fun, I don't care. I'd wear anything that gave me a slight advantage. Trust me, you don't want to give her anything to grab onto, or use against you. She's ruthless and highly skilled." He moves toward me, still speaking to the men. "Last week, my loose tee shirt was whipped over my head—she literally tied me up in it—and smacked my ass. It was humbling, to say the least." He nods toward me, noting my clothing in a head-to-toe appraisal. "So I took a line from her game book and went tight. This snug fabric makes it very hard for her to grasp and grapple. Gives me a better chance of not losing in under five minutes."

We move to the other side of the room, but really there's no lack of space. The inner portion of the dojo could fit three or four sparring pairs, easily. Rafe jumps up and down a few times, stretches his head side to side, and pointedly looks anywhere but at me, while I stare at him intently. My focus never wavers, following his every move while standing perfectly still, my body angled to the side, providing a smaller target.

Without warning, Rafe launches his attack. I side-step, and

execute an arm grab and twist that looks like it's going to break his elbow. Rafe rolls with the arm lock and dives forward, out of my hold. While on the ground, he shifts to deliver a leg sweep, hoping to catch me off guard.

No luck, as I prepared for the move and jump high, pulling my fist back for a blow. As I descend from the jump, my arm ratchets forward, nailing my loving husband in the back of the head.

The blow knocks him flat, a dazed expression on his face. I pause, holding still while watching my opponent for any sign of movement. In a few seconds, Rafe rolls over and gets to his feet, apparently undeterred and looking for more.

"Ready?" I ask.

Rafe nods once, focused on my every move, or lack thereof, a determined look on his face.

"Paul, let's get back to work," Asa says, calling their attention away from us.

The chef's thoughts project across the space, filling my head. *What I'd really like to do is get him to focus on something as intently as she is, then maybe I'd have a chance of catching him off-guard and landing a blow.*

Without dwelling on his words for too long, I get back to the fight with Rafe. If I falter in my concentration to worry about the two of them, my opponent will notice and press his advantage. Sure enough, his fist flies toward me and I barely avoid the blow.

Wow, he's getting faster. Must be the blood.

What color are Paul's shoes? I hear in my head. *What kind of shoes are they?*

A grunt of pain and a solid thump pulls both Rafe and I

around. Elation swells in my mind at the small victory, flooding my body with happiness at the achievement.

"Blue!" Asa yells, falling to one knee. He stands quickly, the surprise etched on his face over Paul landing a solid hit is almost as great as the chef's.

Crap. That's not my elation. It's Paul's.

The fledgling is unknowingly projecting more than just his thoughts—he's nudging Asa's mind with a pointed distraction and broadcasting his emotions, too.

Without communicating an end to our round, we've stopped sparring while my stare fixes on Paul. This is going to require me to do something. Dammit. I really wanted to spar, too. I glance at Rafe, who nods in understanding.

"Paul, my dear, let's have a chat in the hallway."

Oh shit. What did I do?

I resist answering him telepathically, and he follows me out, stopping outside the door to lean against a wall in the hallway. "Is something wrong, Vivian? I thought I was doing pretty good in there. Holding my own for once."

"Hmm... is that what you really think, Paul? Did you use your fighting skills in there, or perhaps something else gave you an advantage?"

"I... uh..." He looks down and jerks when he notices his blue sneakers. I can feel the fear clutching his heart as he realizes what he did. "I didn't mean to!"

I reach a hand to his forearm, my face softening in compassion. "It's okay, Paul. You didn't hurt anyone permanently. But you have to promise me something."

He nods, his posturing and muscles stiffening. I sense he doesn't trust my calm, rational voice as a reality, fearing I'm going to unleash a can of whoop ass on him the likes of which he's never experienced before.

"Relax, I'm not going to hurt you."

Tension slides out of him. "Okay. What do you want me to promise?"

"Don't project thoughts, desires, questions, wants, needs... pretty much anything to anyone, without me there."

"I didn't mean to, I swear!"

"I know, I know, calm down. Sparring is supposed to simulate fighting in real life, and it's only helpful if you practice like it's a real threat. But you still have a lot of the basics to master before you should even consider integrating mind-manipulation into your fighting repertoire."

"I understand what you're saying. But if I don't know when I'm doing it, how can I know to stop?"

"Tell me what you were thinking right before you accidentally projected." I already know the answer, but want him to figure it out.

"Uh..." He stops for a moment, perhaps to gather his thoughts. "I was thinking I wished Asa would be distracted by my shoes. Like he'd glance down and I'd catch him off-guard."

"And is that what happened?"

"Yes, it is. His eyes wavered and I pressed forward with my attack. He then shouted out the color of my shoes after my strike landed."

"Okay, so it sounds like you're going to have to curb your impulses a bit better."

He looks away and mumbles, "Easier said than done."

"I know, Paul. Trust me, I *know*. But you still have to try. If you focus on developing the ability rather than learn concrete fighting techniques, you're going to be screwed in a real physical challenge, you understand?"

"Yeah, I get it. I just don't know how to do it. Can you put a block in my mind, or *suggest* I don't project anymore?"

My face freezes and my good humor slides away. I don't think he fully realizes what he's asking me. To consciously insert a block into someone's mind messes up everything leading to and away from the block. It's risky. And if it's not the last and only option, then it shouldn't be the first choice. "I can, Paul. But that's not a healthy option—for *you*. Why would you ever invite someone into your head to play around?"

He quickly shakes his head. "I didn't mean to. No, definitely not. I suggested it because I trust you. I didn't understand the implications."

"I figured as much. If anything, you need to be working on building your inner walls and safeguards, to *not* allow someone else inside." I smile and draw him back toward the dojo. "One idea could be to wear a lined silver hood. It'll block your abilities."

"Would the silver hurt me?"

"Not as long as it's lined and not touching your skin directly. But more important, is building your control. How about we start working on those blocking techniques right after we finish sparring? No offense, Paul. But it's going to take you years of fight training before you're ready to pit your skills against anyone you might face from the Tribunal or this secret society of manipulators. Protecting your head against enemies is probably the smarter option."

"Okay, great." His head comes up and locks on his training instructor. "Does that mean I can take a break and watch you beat on Asa for a change?"

Asa's gaze is fixed on us. He nods, up to the challenge.

"Sure." I say, glancing at the large, muscular shaved-headed vampire. "That sounds like fun."

A tightening of Asa's jawline lends a determined cast to his expression. "Bring it."

CHAPTER TWELVE: RAFE

Asa steps forward, almost as if he's squaring his resolve, his face settling into a blank mask. He bounces on his toes and side steps, crossing one foot in front of the other, circling the smaller form of my wife, looking for an opening. It's like he thinks controlling his outward appearance will make a difference when going toe to toe with a vampire who can read your mind.

Then again, it's not like Dria needs to slip into his head to beat him, nor would she when sparring. Knowing her, she could probably trounce him blindfolded while wearing a silver hood. I glance once more at his stance. I doubt he's aware of it, but the young man broadcasts his next move, a split second before he acts.

Poor guy. He has no idea what he just opened himself up for.

Dria sees the opportunity and adjusts her response, countering with a solid hit that sends him to the mat. The soldier is like a jack-in-the-box, popping back up, seemingly without effort, to dance the opposite direction.

After a few minutes of attack and smack down, sweat dribbles down his scalp and his fancy footwork from earlier seems to have slowed. I give them another couple minutes and then he'll be done. There's no way he'll be able to last much longer. Hopefully, she won't crush his self-confidence too badly. It's always easier to witness someone else suffer at the hands of a master, rather than endure the beating yourself.

Very soon, the only sound in the still air of the dojo is of Asa's labored breathing, wheezing raggedly in and out. Whoever said vampires don't need to breathe never witnessed one fighting with a master vampire. The sweat I noticed a few minutes ago now drips off his nose. He won't be able to say he didn't get a good work out, that's for sure.

As their sparring continues, Asa begins to shout when executing a move—either as a distraction or in an expression of frustration, I'm not sure. In a series of moves almost too quick to track with the human eye, my wife throws the younger vampire, hard and fast. The thump of his head reverberates through the floor, releasing a pained yell from his lips.

The young man lies in a heap, dazed and slow to react. He grunts and rolls over, not popping up like he did the first few times he went down. "Holy crap. For a tiny thing, you sure do hit hard."

Vivian doesn't respond, just continues to watch him carefully.

I chuckle. "That's the understatement of the year."

Asa glances at me then back to Vivian and scowls. "You don't even look winded."

"But you," she says, "on the other hand, are showing

serious signs of wear. I'd rather not continue and risk you getting injured. Great session, Asa." She smiles with good humor. "You did really well."

He grunts his agreement, looking like he's holding back spewing obscenities. Yeah, I get that. I want to swear at her after we spar, too.

She waltzes out, presumably heading to the showers in the gym locker room like she normally does after practice. Justin appears in the doorway, perhaps drawn by the noise. Asa, still facing the back of the dojo, doesn't notice his presence.

Well, now is as good a time as any for them to meet, right?

"Hey, Asa," I call out. "Got a minute? There's someone I'd like to introduce you to."

He turns toward the door, and sees the tall, lanky stranger. His expression registers confusion and then his mouth drops open and his eyes roll back in his head. The shaved-headed vamp sways forward and crashes to the mat, out like the proverbial light.

Paul's first reaction is to laugh, loud and long, while mine is to rush forward and kneel at the fallen man's side. I gently turn Asa over to face the ceiling and check his vitals. He appears to have fainted, perhaps from the shock of seeing his brother—although I'm sure the blows to the head courtesy of my wife played a large part, too.

"Justin," I say, "Why don't you go take a seat in the dining room? We'll be in to join you once he comes to. I'm sure he just took one punch too many today."

"Do you think he's okay?" the young wizard asks, concern marring his features. "Should we call a doctor?"

"A doctor?" Paul repeats, laughter still tinging his voice. "You do know he's—"

"That's enough, Paul." I cut him off before he reveals Asa's undead condition. Not that it's a secret, but Asa may want to tell him. "Justin was just trying to help." I motion toward the door. "Don't worry, I'll take care of him. He'll be fine."

Justin takes one last look at the prone man on the floor, still having no idea who he is. "Okay. I'll wait for you." But instead of walking out, he steps closer, staring down at his brother. "He looks oddly familiar, but I don't recall meeting him. Was he in Argentina with you?"

Well, this certainly isn't going as planned. "Uh, no. He wasn't. But I'm not surprised he looks familiar."

Justin lifts an eyebrow, "Really? Why?" At my lack of response, he shakes his head. "Yeah, that's not vague or anything." He stands over his brother, contemplating his face. "There's something about him..."

"I'd meant to tell you in another way, so I'm sorry about this." Justin glances up at me, his features questioning. I take a deep breath. "His name is Asa Monson. And we think he's your brother. Eric works here, too."

The wizard's confusion turns quickly to shock. "What? I'm sorry. Did you just say the guy on the floor is my *brother*? As in, from the family I haven't seen for fifteen years? How could that be possible?"

"Vivian has this theory about Fate..." I quickly realize that won't mean shit to a guy his age and change tactics. "We hired Asa last year—through a mutual connection, he came to us when we had a need for more security. A few months later we had a group here from Canada. His brother was with them and they reconnected on the resort.

"I know it's a lot to absorb." I lean down and raise one of Asa's eyelids, checking for a pupil reaction. "Would you mind waiting outside until he wakes up? I don't want to freak him out even more."

"Uh... okay." Justin takes another look at his brother before turning to leave.

In less than a minute, Asa wakes up to the grinning face of Paul, leaning over to see if he's okay. I back up and stand to give them both room.

"He's back," Paul says.

"What the hell happened?" Asa asks, his voice groggy.

"You fainted, man," Paul replies, a tinge of superior-sounding glee in his voice.

Embarrassment heats Asa's face. "No way. I'm not a fainter."

Paul smothers a smile. "Went down like a tree in the woods. Timber!"

I shove Paul out of the way and lean down to help Asa sit up. "Take a few deep breaths."

"I'm pretty sure that's what got me into this mess in the first place. Your wife seriously kicked my ass today."

I examine his face carefully. I don't think he recalls what brought on the faint. "It could have been that, yeah. But I have a feeling it has more to do with who you saw after."

Asa's face scrunches up, like he's thinking back. Then his expression clears and stares at me. "Holy shit. You were with my brother, weren't you? I didn't imagine it, right? Where is he?"

Justin's voice comes from the hall. "Out here, Asa. Don't worry, you're not the only one freakin' out right now." His long-lost brother moves to the doorway.

A shudder runs through Asa. "They told me it might be a possibility..." he says, "but I guess I just didn't believe it."

"You probably figured like I did—what the hell are the chances?"

"Then again, our name isn't very common."

"Wow," Asa says, struggling to stand and waving off my help. "I think I'm still in shock."

I shepherd him out of the room. "Let's get you two a place to sit down."

Paul mutters in the background, "Yeah, before another one falls down."

"Enough, Paul," I say. "Need we remind you of all your weak points since you turned?"

Picturing the last time Paul screamed like a girl and ran out of the room, I smile to myself. And that was just last week.

I walk past his brother, motioning for both of them to follow me. They walk side by side, each of them in their own cloud of shock and disbelief.

"How about the dining room?" I ask. "It should be empty this time of day."

They trail along behind and stand at the table closest to the kitchen, near the back left corner. I slip behind the counter and grab two mugs, glancing their way to make sure they've taken a seat. "How about I whip you both up something to drink?"

Asa extends a hand in greeting, then seems to think better of it and drags the awkward man into a hug. "I wouldn't have believed it, if I hadn't seen you with my own eyes."

"It's really you?" Justin asks. "You remember me and growing up in West Milford, New Jersey?"

They sit at the table, the chaotic energy swirling around them almost palpable. "Of course, man. I'm older but not that old."

"Jesus," Justin says. "I can't believe I'm sitting here with you. This is insane."

"How long has it been?" Asa asks.

"This winter will be sixteen years, right?"

I gather the fixings for hot cocoa, and a bag of blood to spike Asa's mug. I'm sure they could both use the sugar right about now.

"Yeah, I think," he answers. "So, where did you guys go after Jersey?"

Justin's face twists at the memory. "We bounced around quite a bit for the first six months, traveled mostly in the South, lived in the car if we didn't have money for a place to stay. It was hell until mom secured a job out of the country. We moved to Argentina in late spring and the rest is..."

"History?" Asa says with a wry grin.

His brother smiles back, but on his face, it's more of a sardonic grin. "I was going to say complicated and mostly uneventful. It was what it was, you know? Mom was consumed by hate and unhappiness. It was all I could do to keep her on track and responsible. She would have easily slipped into a dark depression by herself."

"You're using past tense when talking about mom—is she gone?"

He nods, some of the good cheer leaving his expression. "She died in a fire."

"Oh." Asa jerks in the chair, seeming off balance at the news.

Justin continues on, unfazed by the topic of their mother's death. "Where did you go after we took off?"

"We never left. Moved to a new house, but always stayed in New Jersey."

A look I can't decipher crosses Justin's expression, but clears in a moment to leave a slight smile. "I never knew. Seems unreal. I—" He hesitates and looks down, his smile fading. "If she wasn't already dead, I'd be so angry at mom right now. You all stayed in Jersey and she made me feel like we could never locate you, like she'd tried and dad took you away or something."

"But *she* took you away from *us*, that makes no sense."

"Yeah, in hindsight, sure. But at the time, she painted a very compelling picture with her words, convincing me the three of you left at the same time and we'd have to save money to hire someone to find you."

Asa shakes his head, anger building and then fizzling out just as quickly. "That sounds like something she'd do," he says, trying careful to sound neutral. "I'm only sorry that I never tried to find you when I turned eighteen."

"Same here," he says.

"Where did mom die?"

"At her house. The official report is an accidental fire, but I've never been so sure."

"What do you think happened?"

"I think she was developing a spell that skirted the line between light and dark a little too close—meaning she shouldn't have attempted it—and the spell backfired on her."

"Whoa. So Mom was a witch? I thought that Wiccan stuff she practiced was safe and non-threatening."

Justin shifts in his chair and glances out the window and then back toward Asa.

"She wasn't a witch. But I do think her eventual exposure to magic was a direct result of her being open to Wiccan philosophies."

"If she wasn't a witch, then how did she do magic?"

"Haven't they told you why I'm here?" Justin asks.

A smile curves Asa's lips. "You haven't had much exposure to Vivian and Rafe yet, but you'll see they don't always reveal all the details to everyone. All I know is you're here to beef up security in ways that I can't. But what more could you do that I can't? Not that I would mind the help, just curious."

"Well, remember how I said Mom practiced magic? She taught me, too. You can learn the craft even if you're not born a witch, but doing so requires a different approach. Anyone not born a witch, but still able to do magic through spells, rituals, and ingredients is called a wizard, or warlock, depending on what you prefer to be called.

"I'm here to set up security wards around the resort's perimeter." He glances at me behind the counter, prepping their drinks, but doesn't elaborate further on what he'll be doing with me. "They'll be triggered when anything crosses over the property line that intends the inn or its inhabitants harm."

Intrigued by the idea, Asa leans forward in his seat. "Interesting. Could I use the same skills to protect the inn? Is it something you could show me?"

Justin hesitates. "I think that's something you'd need to discuss with Rafe. It's not as easy as it sounds."

I approach the table and places two mugs in front of the boys. Sliding one closer to Justin I say, "Hot coco, plenty of sugar, which is good for a shock." The next I push toward Asa, "Ditto for you, but with bagged blood mixed in, too."

Justin looks at Asa curiously, so he leans in and takes the mug, drawing long and deep from the sugary-bloody goodness.

I silently retreat behind the counter and fill a mug for myself from a waiting carafe.

"Damn," Justin says. "It's really true then, huh?"

A bark of laughter escapes Asa. "You caught on to the vampire thing already?"

Justin shrugs in nonchalance. "I worked with the Tribunal in Argentina. Kind of get used to looking for the signs. Pale skin, no recent tan, even in the summer, we're meeting at night... should I go on?"

"Nah, I'm just glad you know. Makes things easier."

"How did it happen?"

"I was attacked after a skirmish in Afghanistan. Most of my unit was killed, and this creature came to prey on those not quite dead."

My brother shakes his head in commiseration. "And that's how it got you, eh?"

"Yeah, but I'm lucky. Not only did it share it's blood and save me, it was within its rights to make me subservient in its seethe. Instead, it left me on my own to die or live."

"That sucks." Seeming to hear what he said after it came out, he smiles. "Literally, eh?"

"Yeah. You get used to it. I'm in a better place now, and it looks like the Fates have conspired to bring the Monson boys back together again."

"How is Eric doing? Hopefully, I'll get to meet him soon."

"He's resilient, like always. Never got over Mom up and leaving with you, but like me, he put it behind him after a while." Asa smiles, a hint of devilment in his eyes. "Did anyone tell you he gets furry at the full moon?"

"Get out!" Justin says with a trace of laughter in his voice. "He's a werewolf? How the hell did that happen?"

"Not just him, Pat Larson, too."

Justin grabs his mug, a grin spreading across his face. "Really? Now this is a story I can't wait to hear."

Just then, my phone vibrates, indicating a text has come in. It's from Diego at the hangar: Lost contact with plane. Awaiting news from Fairbanks.

I slip into our apartment and immediately call. This can't be good.

CHAPTER THIRTEEN: ERIC

When I come to, pain lancing through my awareness, I'm still strapped in my chair. Half of the front of the plane is missing, and I have no idea where Pat and Drew are. My seat lies on its own island of broken plane, no roof or sides around me.

I look over my limbs, checking for injury, and find a jagged piece of metal sticking out of my thigh. As injuries go, it could have been a lot worse. I wonder if I was the one who screamed during the crash.

I fumble for the seat belt catch and unlock it, feeling the painful pull of skin around the leg wound as my weight shifts.

"Pat?" I call. "Are you okay?"

I look behind me, expecting to see the seat he was in, only to find the back half of the plane is missing, too. Shit. It's going to be a bitch getting all those boxes loaded again.

Jesus, listen to me. It's not like we can load them back up and be on our merry way. The plane is literally in pieces. I must be experiencing shock.

"Pat!" I yell louder. Where is that son of a bitch? Warmth from the unrelenting sun of an Alaskan summer beats down on me as I struggle to stand on one leg. I'll have to go find him. I squint while looking around, another thought occurring to me. Where the hell is Drew? He can't tolerate exposure to the sun for long.

I stagger to my feet and gingerly step over the wreckage around me. The bench seat Pat was strapped to isn't far away. I reach it and my spirits plummet. He's not buckled to it, like I was.

My heart begins to pound as I scan the wreckage for signs of him. It looks like the plane twisted in half on the roll, scattering part of the front and rear in opposite directions. The wings being torn off probably helped in halving the aircraft, too. Come on, come on... where is that bastard...

There! Against the tree line, there's something that could be a body.

It takes me longer than I'd like to hobble to the huddled form, but soon I'm hunched over my friend's unconscious face calling his name. Getting no response, I examine him quickly. There aren't any obvious wounds, so hopefully he's got nothing going on internally. "Pat," I try again, softer this time, reaching a hand to his shoulder to gently shake him. "Come on, man. I need you to wake up. We've got a vampire to find."

Pat moans, the low sound releasing a tightness in my chest. Thank God, he's still alive. Supernatural healing doesn't help if you die instantly from a sudden vicious attack. Like a stake to the heart or a severed head. Some things are instant deal breakers, no matter your persuasion.

"What happened?" Pat whispers, his voice a dry croak.

"The engine died and Drew had to crash land the plane."

Pat's eyes flutter open and he takes in our surroundings. "Well, it looks like he did a bang up job on the 'crash' part."

A faint voice sounds from off to my right, the direction where the remains of the front of the plane lie. "Any landing you can walk away from is a good landing."

"Drew?" I call. "You all right?"

Sounds of grating metal and wrenching steel reaches us. "No. I appear to be stuck. Can you help me?"

"Yeah, give me a minute to get there." I look down at Pat, who's checking his limbs and torso carefully for wounds. "Coming with me?"

He tests standing, making it up after two tries. "I think so. No broken bones. How about you?"

I motion down to the metal in my leg. "Looks worse than it is. I think the bleeding has stopped."

"That'll change if you try and remove the steel."

"Yeah, I know. Figured I'd leave it in place for now."

"Good choice. First aid 101. Let's go see how the bloodsucker is doing."

"I can still hear fine," Drew says, a touch of humor lacing his strained voice.

Pat and I work our way slowly through the wreckage to find him. The vampire lies pinned under part of the front of the plane. His sun-suit, for lack of a proper name, is ripped in several places, and the sun beats down on him, frying the exposed skin.

I lunge forward, hampered by my leg wound, but eager to get to him and cover his flesh before the burning gets worse.

"Thought I smelled roasting pork," Pat says.

"Not funny, prick," I bite out, hurrying as best I can,

gritting my teeth through the pain. "He's our friend, or do I need to remind you?"

Pat strides past me, making his way to Drew faster than I can. "Relax, boner. Just trying to add some levity to this shitty situation." He pulls off his shirt and tosses it over the largest area of the vampire's exposed, reddened skin. "Christ, that looks bad. How does it feel?"

Drew's facial covering is torn, too, and what little flesh I see is blistered, and red. "Let's just say it doesn't tickle."

Pat and I work together, as best we can, to lift or drag away the debris covering the vampire. Each piece we remove uncovers more exposed skin to the unrelenting sun overhead.

"He's going to need something to cover him up," I say. "Do you have any ideas?"

Pat tilts his head and stares at Drew. "We could bury him."

"Seriously?" I resist thumping him in the back of the head, but only because he's out of reach. "And what, leave him here 'til winter?"

"Well, how else does a vampire survive in the summer during the day? I think I saw it in a movie once. The vamp was being chased and he had to hide under dirt, leaves, and pine needles until dark."

"Uhh..." I stammer.

"Dude, it worked in the movie."

Drew starts laughing, but it's a dry mirthless kind of sound. Could shit get any worse? Before I have a chance to dwell on exactly how it could, Pat leans down and hoists an arm under our friend. We work together to drag the bleeding, scorched vampire under the shade of the pine trees near the edge of the stream bed. The injured vamp hisses in pain, but otherwise doesn't protest.

"I think both my legs are broken," he reports when we ease him down to the ground.

"Allow me to point out the obvious," Pat says. "That's gonna hinder us greatly in attempting to walk back to safety. How about we call for help?"

"Good idea, except the control panel held the radio," Drew replies.

"Yeah? So? Should I go look for it?"

"That was the burning hunk of twisted scrap you pulled me out from under. And besides, we're too far past Fairbanks' reach, and not close enough to the inn's. "

"What about the satellite phone?" I ask. "They're in every plane on the resort. That's got to work."

Pat spends a few minutes searching for it, only to discover its crushed case and broken contents. "Shit. We're screwed."

Drew waves him back to the shade. "No, we're not, and don't panic, Pat. Once we miss arrival time, flight service from Fairbanks will call the inn and they'll start a search."

"Oh yeah, won't that just be great," my friend replies. "They'll bundle up our fried vampire and whisk him away to a hospital for proper care." He motions to the metal in my leg. "And how the hell are we going to explain your speedy healing once they get that out? We're so screwed. Vivian is going to be pissed."

Despite the pain and blood loss, I'm feeling annoyed. "Seriously? We survive a wicked plane crash and you're blathering on about how pissed our boss will be?" I shake my head, trying to clear my thoughts. "You're unbelievable sometimes, dude."

"What? You think she's going to be happy we called attention to an injured vampire? Especially with all that's going on? No need to worry about the nut-jobs in Argentina blowing it for supernaturals, we'll do it all by ourselves."

"Like a wounded vampire has never been accidentally taken to a hospital before? He can just mind-control them, you idiot."

"Stop bickering," Drew says with a slight wheeze, followed by a grimace of pain. "We're going to start walking. As soon as my legs work."

"How long will it take you to heal?" I ask Drew, hoping we can get moving soon.

"Pretty quick with an infusion of fresh blood." He raises his eyebrows under the rips in his facial covering. "Any volunteers?"

Silence from Pat and me. All the times we've gone flying with Drew, somehow being his emergency snack never occurred to me.

"Any chance we were bringing back a shipment of blood in the plane?" Pat asks, a twitter of fear lacing his voice.

"Come on, guys. I'm not going to drain you dry for crying out loud. But if you want me to help walk back to civilization, one of you is going to need to donate to the cause."

"Shit," Pat says.

"That seems to be your favorite word today," I say in a light voice.

"And what the fucking hell if it is?" The young werewolf waves his arms around. "We've just crashed a fucking PLANE. Don't you think someone with long red hair is going to be really fucking pissed we destroyed her plane?" He's apparently on a roll, because he starts to flail his arms more wildly. "Look at us. Look at this shit. We are FUCKING screwed, Eric!"

The voice of reason comes from Drew this time. "You obviously don't know our master well."

Pat whips around to stare at him. "She's not my master. Not technically, at least. And what's that supposed to mean?"

"To borrow from your vocabulary, she won't give a shit about the fucking plane. It's money. Easily replaceable. All she'll care about is if we made it out alive."

Pat takes a deep breath. The tension visibly leaving his body. "Oh. Are you sure?"

"Yes. Now give me your wrist, you stinky bastard."

The volatile werewolf saunters closer, his swagger back now that his immediate fear has been addressed. "Dude, that's not how you butter up a date."

"You're not a date. You're a snack. Either that, or you can carry my broken body back to the inn and explain to Vivian why you wouldn't help heal me."

Pat immediately steps forward and kneels next to the prone vampire under the shady tree branch, offering his wrist. "No need to get hasty, you fanged bugger. Here."

I move forward to offer my own wrist, but Drew waves me back, gesturing with his chin toward my leg. "We'll be doing something for you next."

And with that vague statement, he grabs Pat's wrist and draws it toward his mouth. He bites cleanly and quickly, pulling sustenance eagerly from my friend's veins.

"This is really gross," Pat says within the first few seconds, but very quickly, his face changes and you can tell it's not as bad as it once was. "Okay. Now I get the appeal. It's starting to feel really good. Oh.... No." His face scrunches up. "A bit too good."

I laugh, despite the danger we're in. My old friend is crossing his legs and looking uncomfortable.

"Dude, how much longer?" he asks the suckling vampire. "I'm ready for you to stop."

Drew doesn't answer, he keeps his mouth latched around the wound he made. After another minute he draws away, not a drop of blood spilling out to be wasted.

"Your turn," the semi-satiated vampire says, motioning to me. He pats the ground next to him. "Sit here."

"Sitting is kind of hard with this damn thing in my leg."

Without warning, Drew's hand flashes out and grabs the ragged piece of steel sticking out of my thigh. In one shift move he pulls it out, drawing an unexpected scream of agony from my lips.

"Fuuuccckkk!" I screech, the pain so strong I fall on my way to the ground. "What the hell are you doing?"

Drew doesn't reply, he just tears his teeth across the skin on his wrist and thrusts it toward me. "Drink one mouthful."

"That's it!" Pat yells. "I'm outta here." The squeamish werewolf leaves the cover of the shade and storms toward the smoking plane wreckage.

Drew hasn't taken his eyes off me. "Do it. It'll help you heal faster. And there's no way we're getting out of here quickly with you on one leg."

Disgust roiling in my middle, I lean forward, and place my mouth over his wound. I pull in one mouthful of his sickly sweet and salty blood, forcing my gag reflex back. I swallow it, and instantly feel the magic from his blood filling my body. The pain in my leg subsides as his stronger blood helps the accelerated healing process werewolves already possess.

The blood seeping slowly out of the fresh wound stops, and in a few more minutes my leg is completely healed.

The power contained in the vampire's blood doesn't stop with the healing of my leg. The surge of strength and the feeling I can accomplish anything fills me, compelling me to get up, to DO something, to do anything rather than sit here. "That's some good shit you've got there," I say, a slight slur in my voice.

"You don't need much to aide your lycan healing abilities."

"So I gathered." I stand and test my weight on the leg. All's good. "What's next?"

"Next, we call back Pat and devise a plan."

"Sounds good." I lurch forward, using my arms to clear away the branches hampering my view. "Jackass!" I call to my best friend. "Where are you?"

"Are you two done with your 'moment'?" Pat yells from the broken luggage compartment in the hull.

I leap, covering the distance from the tree to the plane in one bound. I stick my head through a jagged opening in the metal hull to see what he's doing.

"Boo!" I call out, hoping to surprise him.

Pat jerks slightly and looks up, cocking an eyebrow. "What the hell's up with you? What are you, ten?"

"I feel really good, man. Like really good. Invincible good. Leg's good as new." To punctuate my healthiness, I punch a fist through the steel next to me.

"And... I think you're a little high from the blood. Calm down and make it last. We've got a long trip back."

A hopeful lilt comes into my voice. "Does that mean you've figured out where we are?"

"Not quite. I've been thinking about when we left, how

long we traveled before the malfunctions hit, and where we might be."

"What did you determine?"

"That we're screwed, just like I said. A half hour by plane covers a shit-load of territory, especially up here in no man's land."

A thought occurs to me and I dig out my cell phone. No service, of course. "Damn it. There goes my one bright idea."

"If a cell phone hundreds of miles from a cell tower is your bright idea, then you need a better imagination."

I shove him playfully across the debris field back to our friend sitting in the shade, and duck under the branches.

"Ah, you found him," Drew says.

"Yeah, not like he could have gone far. So what's next? How are you feeling?"

"I'm good to go. The minor wounds have all closed and internally I'm no longer hemorrhaging."

"Internal bleeding? You can tell that kind of thing?"

Drew raises a shoulder. "You learn more about your body and how things work over many, many years of existence. I had pain, I knew it needed to heal, I got blood—all healed. Pretty simple."

I motion to the large tears in the stretchy fabric covering his legs, torso, and arms. "You can't see it, but the back is worse. How are you going to survive the sun?"

"I have an idea," Pat says, dashing back to the scattered boxes, opening them one by one. "Aha! Diane bought some new clothes this time. Let's see what we can do to protect him from the sun."

Pat returns, carrying two pairs of jeans. "Let's wrap these

around you and see if it's enough to block out the sun. Give me your paracord bracelet, Eric."

"Why?"

He draws out a knife from his pocket. "So I can cut up the jeans and then tie them around him, using the rope to keep the material in place."

"Good idea. And then what?" I ask, slipping the bracelet over my hand. "We walk home?"

"Do you have a better plan?"

"Nope."

"Well, then. Walking it is."

CHAPTER FOURTEEN: VIVIAN

I stride into the conference room, glancing around to make sure everyone has arrived. Justin sits next to his brother, Asa, and only then can I see a slight family resemblance, mostly around the eyes and jawline.

"Reports. Where are we with locating the plane?" My eyes shift to Asa.

"Diego reported losing contact with the plane approximately an hour outside Fairbanks. At that time, if they'd gone down, they'd be close to two hundred miles from Deadfoot."

"*If?*" I ask. "Aren't we sure the plane has crashed?"

Asa nods. "We are now, but when we first lost contact we had no way of knowing exactly *when* they went down."

Rafe asks the next question that popped to my mind, too. "What about the emergency beacon in the plane? Isn't there some kind of tracking system in place?"

"Yes, and they'd be aware of it." Asa's frustration spills out. "But they'd also know that a crash means search parties from

Fairbanks would be on their way— where they'd find two werewolves and a vampire—who may or may not be injured. With luck, they'll realize it and leave."

"What are you implying?" Justin asks. "Why would them being supernaturals make them less likely to stay for help?"

Rafe answers before I can. "They're smart. If they haven't stayed with the crash, it's for a reason. Like perhaps they have injuries that could reveal their true nature."

Paul asks, "Is there any way to determine how the plane went down? Or why?"

"Not yet," Asa says. "At least, I don't think there is and Diego hasn't mentioned anything. Maybe the on-site team would be able to figure it out after studying the wreckage."

Paul persists, "Isn't there a black box thingy that may help?"

"Sure. It'll help—eventually. But not in locating them." Asa looks at the chef with renewed interest. "Why? What are you thinking?"

"The timing feels off." Paul glances down at his hands on the table, unwilling to meet the staring eyes around the table. "We've got a lot of threats facing us already, you know? I'm wondering if the plane going down was an accident or planned."

The room falls silent at his suggestion.

My voice comes out calmer than I feel. "Are you suggesting sabotage, either internally or externally from an enemy?"

Paul snorts. "Internally, really? Who the hell on the resort would sabotage our only way to get mail? And, let's face it, we have more planes. It's not like breaking one would inhibit us from leaving."

Justin raises a hand to speak. "Don't kill the messenger, but if this was external sabotage, wouldn't it have to be committed by someone internal, like here on the resort?"

"That's a possibility," Asa says with a grimace. "Not an attractive one, but a possibility nonetheless. But couldn't the plane have been tampered with at the airport in Fairbanks?"

I tap my fingers on the table, my nerves getting the better of me at the talk of sabotage. "How long are they normally on the ground with the plane unattended?"

"Is it really unattended with Drew there?" Rafe asks. "Does he leave the plane when Pat and Eric go to get the mail? It is mid-day sun, after all. Wouldn't he stay in the dark hangar?"

"Yeah," Asa says. "That would be my guess, too."

Jon stands and starts to pace. Dammit, he beat me to it. Now I'll just have to sit here and stew. "Then we're back to square one, aren't we? We have to find them and hear what they have to say."

"All right then," Jon says while walking circles around the table. "Working on the assumption they did not stay at the plane's crash site for a search party to find them, they would be walking home—on foot—right?"

Nods around the table confirm we're all thinking along the same lines. "Okay then, let's do some guesstimating. How far is Fairbanks from here and what's a rough estimate on how far they could have flown before we lost contact with them?"

Asa types furiously on the tablet in front of him. "Fairbanks is close to three hundred miles from the resort, and they could have traveled over a hundred miles in the time they were airborne." He pulls up a map and circles the range with the tip of a finger. "That means they could be possibly injured and attempting to walk over a hundred and fifty miles—through woods, over streams, elevation changes, and with no real break from the sun for close to twenty hours—to make it here."

"Do you have the search area mapped out?" I ask, leaning forward to look at his screen.

"For the most part. Based on what we've got so far for intel. But it's a shit load of area to cover. I'm not sure how much you expect us to get done in one day, even with all of us searching."

Rafe's fingers drum on the table. "I've been thinking along the same lines. Let's try and narrow down the search radius. If you were them what would you do?"

Jon pauses his pacing and returns to his seat. "That's a good question.... If it was me, I'd be trying to get as close to civilization as I possibly could. Especially if I wasn't sure anyone was looking for me."

Asa nods his agreement, interjecting, "I'm with you. Let's just say, worst case scenario, the plane is unsalvageable, the radio doesn't work, nor do their satellite phones, but they're alive. Assumptions being what they are, I realize this is a lot of guessing, but if I was them, I'd be hightailing it as far from the crash site as possible, as quickly as I could. So where would you go next?"

"A road," Jon says. "Or a village. I'd walk toward civilization of some kind. What do you think?"

"If it were me," I say. "I'd walk to the closest road. Assuming I wasn't so blood-starved I was a danger to whomever stopped to help."

Rafe reaches out a hand and rubs my back, sensing my growing tension. "I think you're on the right track. Haul Road. That would be the way to go."

Asa glances back at his tablet, "So we should focus on the area around Haul Road? That's still over a hundred miles."

Justin grabs a sheet of paper and starts scribbling. "Not when you narrow it to how far they can walk per hour, through the woods, and calculate the distance from our estimation of where the plane went down."

I nod, thinking about all the various vehicle types we have on the property. "This sounds like a good job for the helicopter."

"We have a helicopter?" Paul asks. "So cool."

Rafe nods. "We don't have much need for it—it's an old military surplus item, decommissioned after war time and repurposed for civilian use—but it's here as an emergency. And if this doesn't qualify as one, then I'm not sure what would."

"Where is it?" Asa asks.

"It's in the furthest hangar at the airstrip, the smaller one we use for storage, under a tarp, and it'll need a thorough once over before taking air."

"Who can fly it?" Paul asks.

Rafe raises and hand and points a finger at me then Jon while speaking, "I can fly it, as can Viv, Jon, Drew, Diego and a few other pilots we have on staff, but most of them are away for the summer. Jon, reach out to Diego to prepare the bird, and we'll take off as soon as it's ready to go."

Jon nods and takes out his phone. "Will do."

"Okay," I say, "now that we've got that covered, where are we with the journals?"

Asa looks down at his notepad. "I've got the first dozen done and estimate it will take me at least two more days to finish the rest. It would go faster with help."

"Okay," I say with a smile. "I'll help while the copter is getting prepped."

Asa's face remains neutral, but it's a safe guess he was probably hoping the help would come from another direction. "And there's more good news on that front. I saw portraits in the journals. Our hope is facial recognition software might be able to help us track your turns down."

I nod, surprised I thought to include a drawing of the vampires I created. If the likenesses are close enough, that could be a big help in finding people. I wonder if seeing the pictures would help trigger memories for me? I'll have to test the theory later.

Continuing with my internal list of what to touch base on, I look toward Justin and Rafe. "Where are we with the new security wards?"

My husband responds, "We've completed half the circumference of the property so far. We'll start on the next section in the morning."

"Okay, good. How about a tracking spell tuned to Eric? Could you manage that, Justin? I'm happy to give you more of my blood if you need it."

"A tracking spell? Yeah, I can do that. I'll get right on it after the meeting. It'll be ready before morning."

"Will you need something from Eric?"

"I could make one without it, but yeah, if you could get me hair from a brush, that would make it more powerful."

Rafe picks up his phone and starts typing. "I've notified housekeeping. They'll meet you outside of his cabin to let you in."

I nod and turn to our favorite werewolf. "Jon, where are you on mastering your new skill?" I know I'm putting him on the spot with talking about it in front of everyone, but we've got to be ready, and I have no idea when an attack will come, or if the plane crash is indicative that an attack has already begun.

Jon grimaces before replying. "I spent hours on half-shifting this morning and have been able to successfully call forth a full wolf-man shape a few times. I wouldn't say I've mastered it yet, far from it, but I will keep at it and then attempt to teach others when I have."

"Good. When we go hunting my turns, it'll be you, me, and Rafe only. I need each of us to be up to our fighting best." I drum my fingers on the table, my earlier conversation with the doctor coming back to me. "One last thing. Rafe, I need you to issue a mandatory 'vacation' to all the employees. I want every human removed from the resort as soon as possible." A coldness seeps into my heart. My last request is in preparation for war—which is an unwelcome truth I'd prefer to ignore.

Rafe's eyes hold a sadness in them, he knows what the admission will cost me. "Are you sure, liebling?"

"Without a doubt." I steel my spine and rise. "Let's get back to work, people. No one will die on my watch."

CHAPTER FIFTEEN: RAFE

After the status meeting ended, and I sent a text and email to the employees with the good news of their upcoming paid holiday, I finally have a chance to sit down in our office with the journal files. I run the program macros to find key words that might indicate a vampire turning, and instantly, the results appear.

Excitement, anticipation, and tension coils in my middle for a unique and uncomfortable feeling. On the one hand, I'm curious to see what's in the journals. On the other, I worry. I know my wife hasn't purposefully hidden anything from me, and I've certainly seen my share of horrors in her head whenever she's deep in a restorative sleep, but what if what I find here is more than what I expect?

Could she have mass-murdered children simply because she was hungry? What if she mind-raped and abused innocents for centuries and only recently gained a conscience? The unsettling train of thoughts brings a sourness to my gut.

I know my wife. There's no way she's worse than what I

know of her. No one could completely change themselves by willing memories away, could they?

Guilt swamps me, stifling the sick feelings. This is *my wife* we're talking about. I'd give my soul for her.

Taking a deep breath, I shore up my confidence and read the words on the screen.

Last night I turned my lover, Tobias. He was dying slowly of consumption and begged me to save him. I wonder if I've done the right thing. I never changed Charles, despite the many hours we talked about it, because I wasn't sure this cursed existence was a suitable alternative to death and an eventual rebirth. In the end, my second husband died to free me.

I wasn't ready to lose another lover this time. Did I do the right thing? Will I have the courage to kill him if he can't handle the blood lust? Time will tell. And thanks to this never-ending curse, time is one thing I have plenty of.

Okay, so we've got a Tobias here in... what was the date of this entry? I scan back a few pages to find the date, jotting notes on a yellow pad lying on the desk, and then scroll further back to get all the details I can uncover about Tobias, like where they lived at the time, his full name, and anything relating to a physical description of the man.

When I look it over, I realize it's not much data to go on. How the hell is a few lines of info enough to track someone four hundred years later? I wonder if the only way we're going to find these vamps is to force Vivian to remember what happened. She knows what they look like. She could draw us a picture. Then again, with the advent of plastic surgery, anyone in this century who's still around could easily have changed their appearance, permanently.

And if that's the case, then there's no reason to force her to remember. Which once again, leads this entire journal-reading-task back to me.

Resigned to my duty, I flip forward a few more pages, looking for any indication she may have either killed Tobias or set him free. After a dozen pages or so, I hit pay dirt. There's a detailed sketch of a man's face taking up an entire page. Despite it being in black and white, it's incredibly life-like. If Asa could use this with a facial recognition program, we might have a better chance of locating the guy—assuming the vamp is still walking upright.

Giddy with the new-found course for identification, I continue searching.

Tonight, I overfed and almost killed a young man. I couldn't stop myself. And because of my greed, his life would have ended there in my arms, unless I fixed the error and turned him. So I did. I didn't know him. I'd never seen him before tonight. He was a young man, dying in my embrace because I'd waited too long between feedings.

He wouldn't have survived without my interference, the same as he wouldn't have died without it, either. I know this. I know what I did was wrong, but killing him, letting his life slip away while I watched, would have been much worse. Will he make it? Will he be able to survive as a fledgling and control himself?

Or will I have to kill him? All because I lacked control. Stupid slip! And one I will never allow myself to make again. If I turn someone ever again it will be by choice, not because I messed up.

My weakness is inexcusable. I must build safeguards to ensure I never, ever, make the same mistake again.

I skim a few pages forward and see she did indeed have to end the young man's life within two weeks. The entries leading up to his death were long and filled with self-loathing. She clearly hated herself for what she did and for how she tried to remedy the problem.

Her later entries showcase self-destructive behavior, chronicling her brushes with death, severe depression, and self-loathing over the outcome of the young man. It takes many months before an upward tone is visible in her writing, indicating she took a long time punishing herself before she would allow herself to heal, accept, and move forward, and then slowly, methodically, clear her mind of the memories of the life she ended.

And now I'm seeing a pattern to the "rules" in the front of her journal. She created her own standards to live by. As a way to protect whomever donated blood to her from suffering her fate.

At times, I can see that she hated her very existence, but at others, she appears to embrace the power and strength, and realizes she can still do good, even if she drinks blood.

No closer to finding a viable candidate to track, I jump to the next search.

I turned a young, idealist priest today. He was beaten, robbed, and near death when I discovered him in the defiled church. The invaders didn't care if he was a man of the cloth. They didn't care that his church should have been a sanctuary. They left him for dead, after stealing the sparse tithings the poor church collected.

I hesitated before deciding to save him. It took me a long time to make the decision, so long the choice was almost gone. I promised myself if he was horrified by his new existence I would grant him a swift and painless true death. We'll have a lot to overcome if Father Lucas does decide to continue living as a blood drinker. But I knew him well. I watched him grow from a child into an adult. I saw him become a man of honor in the community, one who never turned away someone in need.

And as far as I'm concerned, the world still needs him. Please God, if you're listening, grant me the strength to lead your shepherd to another phase of his life. One that can still include a life of doing good deeds for others—as long as he doesn't get too hungry and suck the parishioners dry.

A priest! Intrigued, I continue reading, hoping he was one of the ones who made it. There's a sketch here as well, and no further entries cataloging his demise. Hopefully this will be someone we find on our journey. Surely a man of God would see the inherent need to stop vampire rule in Buenos Aires. Guess we'll find out when we locate him.

I turn back to my task, heartened we have at least one prospect so far.

Last week, I turned a child. She was twelve and full of life, I couldn't bear to see her destroyed by a vampire who preferred child lovers. The ancient bastard drank her down, with no regard for what he took, no care if she died on the cold marble floor of the Tribunal. He tossed her limp form aside like a rag doll.

He needs to die. I will find a way, mark my words. I will kill that man. Ancient or not, there are some abominations that have no right to live—and he's one of them.

My heart clutches in my chest as I read. I know how this child vampire will turn out. Mikov may not have stressed to her the dangers of turning a child, but Dria has expressed it to me many times in the past. I scan the next few pages, looking for what I know will be there.

After four months of entries, I finally uncover what I feared. The tearful recounting of how she had to kill the creature the little girl had become. I read further to confirm my suspicions, and see exactly what I thought I'd find. This turning, she did not will herself to forget.

This one, she allowed to stay with her.

Forever.

So that she would never make the mistake again.

I fell in love with a pirate. Perhaps it sounds like an adventure one might read about, and at the time, it certainly seemed like one. But the day came when I had to make a choice, I had to choose to let him live forever in his prime, or be taken down by an invader's cutlass. And there were no doubts in my mind that eventually he would've succumbed to the fate of other pirates—death or imprisonment. There aren't many pirates who manage to retire and live off their collected booty, no matter how many sailors dream that's the life that awaits them.

When I turned him, I thought we'd beat the odds. I allowed myself to forget. I wanted to believe we'd make it. That somehow, we'd succeed where other bonded mates turned into vampire couples had failed. We'd make it work. We'd be together forever.

But we didn't. In only six months, I couldn't handle watching him quench his thirst with every pretty woman that crossed his path. It was like a knife twisting in my heart when he'd glamour another wench and suck and fuck his way to satiation.

Despite the ability to drink and walk away. An option he was too uninterested in to try. Even if he could have resisted the temptation, he chose not to.

Never again. We've parted ways and he's living on his own. He is one turn I will gladly wipe from my mind. Marrying a pirate and granting him immortality was the biggest mistake I ever made. To lose my heart and walk away was the greatest pain I've suffered since Charles's death, my second husband who sacrificed himself so I could live free of Mikov's tyranny.

This latest entry clears up the origin of Dria's lingering doubts about whether we could make it or not as a vampire couple. She's told me repeatedly how two vampires can't stay bonded to each other, that it never works. I often wondered if she knew from personal experience, or was it just something she'd been told over and over again.

Thankfully, there's a sketch of him as well. I note the page, skipping back pages to note his given name was Samuel, and jump forward to the next search response.

Virginia was a beautiful young woman. But even if she'd been plain and drab, it wouldn't have made a difference. Those stupid townsfolk had her strung up and ready to burn without even hearing her side of the story. They thought they had the right because she's a witch. Their ignorant, hate-filled faces leered and jeered, practically cheering for her death.

Who does that? I know I broke the one and only rule Mikov said should never be broken. Never turn a witch. How bad could it really be? She's not even twenty years old. There's no way she's some angry, powerful witch I have to worry about going crazy and seeking revenge on the townspeople who tried to kill her.

She's still innocent enough to forgive. To move forward and live her new existence with goodness and discipline. I will not fail her.

I'll watch her longer. I'll keep her with me for a year or more if I have to. I won't unleash a vampire-witch with uncontrollable blood lust on the population of New England. This is my first turn in the new country, and I will ensure my rule-breaking doesn't lead to dire consequences.

Holy shit.

Dria created a vampire-witch, who may very well have become a manipulator at some point after she left. She may have unknowingly created the very thing the Atlantis vampires feared beyond anything else—a vampire with the ability to manipulate their fellow undead, but who was also a witch who could control the elements and nature.

My heart hammers in my chest. I'm not sure what to do or say. I write everything down that might help us find this powerful vampire, not looking forward to when I have to share what I've found with my beloved. She doesn't remember. She's not to blame.

She turned each of them, knowing exactly what she was doing. How is this one any different?

Because this one, this one could change the world.

Feeling energized, I glance at the time. It's getting late. Eager to continue our mate bond ritual, I leave the office and return to our living room, seeking my wife. There's a lot to share with her, but it can keep until she's satisfied and happy.

D ria lies stretched out on our couch, a white terry cloth robe wrapped around her, staring at a candle burning on a side table. There's a hint of shadow in my wife's brilliant green eyes, making me worry she's thinking too much. She's done this before, through the years, where she spends a very long time in meditation to clear her mind. Whenever we face danger, she obsesses about what's to come, and what she can do to plan for every scenario that comes to mind.

Since we've made our seethe larger, she has more people to care about. Which equates to more people to worry about, and ultimately more people to keep safe.

She may come across as an independent, strong-willed, demanding individual. But what she truly is, is far beyond what most of us can accept or even understand.

Dria is a protector, in the truest sense of the word. She is a defender of the weaker people in her sphere. She alone stands between those she loves and the darkness beyond, and if that darkness dwells inside her, then she is in essence guarding us from herself.

As her mate, lover, and husband, I am the one who must protect *her*. Even if that means protecting her from herself.

"Come with me, liebling. It's time for rest." I smile, adding warmth and desire to my expression. Because I know if my words can't make it through to her, I'll have to use every available attribute, including a physical seduction.

She's nothing if not a predictable creature. Vampires are by nature, driven by their desires, their wants, their bodily needs. Even when they don't want to admit it.

"Shall I carry you?" I raise my eyebrows.

A smile, slow to form, stretches across her face. "You sneaky devil, what do you have in mind?"

"Me? Nothing too drastic I assure you. But what I do know is you're driving yourself too hard and you've not had a restorative sleep in days. You push too hard, Dria. If you're not careful our greatest defense will become our greatest weakness."

"I hate it when you're right. And if I say no? Are you to drag me off to our room and put me to bed like a bad little girl?"

The tilt of her chin suggests she's teasing me, pushing to see how far I'll go before I act. "Do you really want to test me?"

Without another word, my wife gets up and saunters toward me.

"I can smell your desires, Rafe," she says in passing. "You obviously have more in mind than me sleeping."

"You've got me. But with your vampire super-smell it's not really much of a challenge, is it?" My eyes linger on her tight butt covered by the robe as she walks through the kitchen, heading straight for our bedroom.

She doesn't answer, nor does she say another word until we get into our room, where she shuts the door behind me and settles at the small sitting table. "Okay, spill it. What's on your mind?"

I settle onto the club chair closest to her and reach out take her hand. "We've got a lot on us. Increasing our security measures, learning new skills, and basically prepping for a war where we have no idea how many challengers we'll face.

"And then there's the big elephant in the room that we haven't talked about— Jon's girlfriend?" Dria's eyes light up. "I think I saw her today. After Justin and I finished, I drove up to check on preparations for the jet, and a woman passed in Jon's truck—a woman I didn't recognize."

My wife's hand stiffens in mine. "Really? Are you sure it wasn't an employee's relative or friend come to visit?"

"I thought that could be an option at first, but why would Jon lend his car to a visitor? We've sensed he's involved with someone. You haven't wanted to talk about it before, but we need to. What do you plan to do before we leave?"

"You know, I've been wondering the same thing. Do we wait until he says something to us? I mean, it's not like we don't know. Perhaps he's waiting for a reason? Maybe to make sure she's the one? Taking a mate certainly shouldn't be rushed. What do you think we should do? Do we barge in and drill him for information? I've been following a wait-and-see attitude to let him have space, to figure out what he really wants. Without our interference."

"That's all fine and dandy in a perfect world, but we are in far from ideal conditions. We're about to leave on a lengthy journey. One that promises to be dangerous for all involved. Do we wait and allow them to mate and then bring her with us? Is there some type of lengthy mating ritual or ceremony between Weres we don't know about? I'm out of my element here."

"I am too. I know what you mean. And I'm not sure what the answer is or what to do." She squeezes my hand as her eyelids lower, a seductive glint in her sparkling green depths. "But surely that can't be the only reason why you were so adamant with wanting me to come rest."

"You're right, there is. We need to do the ritual again tonight."

"We could wait. It doesn't *have* to be every day."

"Don't give me problems about this. We talked it over last night. In addition to you being at your highest strength and getting the restorative sleep you need, we also need *us* to be the strongest that we can be before heading into battle."

And with that I draw my hand back from my wife's and slowly begin to unbutton my shirt. Dria's eyes travel to the skin revealed, her gaze lingering on my fingers. I know she's thinking about how those same fingers played over her body last night, before she once again escaped sleep to leave our bed and pace, determined to hash out a plan. But the responsibility should never be hers alone, it should always fall to us both.

"Turn your mind off for a night, Dria."

Her gaze shifts up to meet mine. "Easier said than done."

"We have no idea what we're facing, right? How much planning can we do? We've got the new members of the seethe training, honing their fighting skills, sharpening the blade, so to speak. All of us need to be at the top of our game. Including you."

I stand and lift Dria from the chair, depositing her curvy form on our bed. I climb in on my knees, stretching out alongside her. My hand slowly trails up my wife's thigh, stroking the exposed skin revealed by her open robe. "Okay, I understand the training aspects of things. And I know I agreed last night, but why rush the bond now? Why go through seven days of intense blood exchange when we need to be getting airborne soon? I worry about the time commitment."

I tamp down my feelings of exasperation, worry, and fear. Putting on a strong face, I lay out why I want to do this. "I believe it will matter. I'm not sure why. Maybe, to make us stronger? Maybe, to increase our bond for long-distance communication?" Shaking my head slightly, trying to dispel unfamiliar insecure feelings, I continue, "I may not be able to put it into words well, but something inside me says this is important, and no—this isn't a ploy to mark you or anything."

Dria's eyebrows raise. "Oh, really? So visiting my old lovers and old turns hasn't got you upset or worried?"

"Are you teasing me, or implying I have a reason to be worried?"

A smile spreads across my wife's face. "I'm teasing you, silly. You've got to be the least jealous person I've ever met my life. Well, unless it comes to Jon."

I shift a little on the bed, my unease giving me away. It's not that I'm jealous of Jon, per se, as it's more I want him more than I'm comfortable with.

Maybe my subconscious hope is to build the bond stronger between Dria and me to make sure he can't get in? God, I hate to think that of myself. After sixty-five years of marriage, have I somehow become this needy man who doesn't trust the relationship I have with my wife?

Shake off the stupid. This is not me. I know my wife. I know our life, and I know my place in both. And whether or not Jon is there next to us doesn't make a difference. In fact, I think we're stronger with him by our side.

Without warning, I pin Dria to the bed. A squeak of interest and amusement sounds from her. "Oh, aren't you the feisty one tonight."

I stifle a smile as I lean down to trail kisses along her neck, my tongue easing out to moisten her skin before each kiss. "I want to taste you, liebling. It's been a long time."

Her chuckle, seductive and warm, reaches my ear. "I can think of several things I'd like you to taste."

As I continue to plant kisses, one hand creeps lower to the

junction between her thighs, applying pressure, adding to her already hot core. "You want my mouth here, liebling?"

She moans and lifts her hips from the mattress, circling slowly in search of more pressure. Wetness escapes her moist folds, dampening my fingers and encouraging me to plunge inside. "You want this, don't you?" I say as I curve my fingers inward. "You want something, don't you?"

Dria's hands flutter against my chest, grasping my shirt front and releasing. She abandons my clothing and opens the tie on her robe instead, parting the terrycloth fabric to bare her newly washed skin to me. Unwilling to hold back my own desires any longer, I succumb to what we both want, and plunge my fingers deep inside her inviting warmth.

A sigh escapes her as her inner muscles clench around the firm digits. Her back arches from the bed, her hardening nipples begging to be tasted, laved, and suckled. I continue my kisses down her neck to her bare breast, capturing her right nipple and drawing it deep into my mouth.

"When you start nice and slow, I know it's going to be a spectacular evening."

I reach for the knife I placed earlier on the bedside table, and nick the skin near the tip of her breast. As my mouth latches over the wound, I draw deeply and project into her mind, *Say the words, my love.*

"My life is your life..."

CHAPTER SIXTEEN: JON

I jolt awake as the last ripples of a massive orgasm seep into my underwear. Extreme satiation fills me, stretching inside to fill every limb. As the warm glow encases me, I feel confused.

What the hell just happened? How am I wearing underwear? Why is it dark all of a sudden? Where are Vivian and Rafe?

Holy crap. It was all a dream.

It felt real. I was there, in their bed. I felt everything.

I ease up the sheet and slide out of bed, unwilling to wake Candy as she slumbers beside me. A glance at the bedside clock reveals that even though it's daylight outside, it's still not morning yet.

Shaking my head, I try to regain a sense of real and unreal. God, what the hell was that? How could I get pulled into one of their dreams? Or was it my dream and I didn't know it? I mean, I haven't had detailed sexual dreams like that about both them in the past.

Wouldn't I know if it was my dream? Jesus, this feels insane. I stand, feeling wide-awake and energized despite it being hours before dawn. There's no getting back to sleep now.

One thing I know for sure, it's too damn early with no coffee in me to be considering such bullshit. I pad softly to the bathroom, take a quick shower, and get dressed. When I return to the bedroom, Candy's still sleep. Good. I think I need to be by myself a little while.

Might as well head up to the hanger and see if I can help Diego with prepping the helicopter. That way, we can get in the air and searching for them as soon as possible. With a course of action laid out for me, I move to the kitchen, make myself a cup of instant coffee, pour it into a travel cup, write a note for Candy, and leave.

Within minutes, I'm pulling my truck into our airport's small parking lot. I enter the small domed hanger to find Diego hard at work.

"Hey, man," I call out. "I came by to see if I can help."

"Great," he says, sliding out from under the bird. "You sure as hell can." Diego stands and motions to the door. "Want to get started with inside? Clean out the cabin and refresh any supplies we might need."

"Can-do." I stride over to the metal shelves lining the walls and grab a garbage bag, Windex, and paper towels before returning to the copter. The work is tedious, but I don't mind. Keeps my mind off the threesome I just dreamed about.

Of course, after a few minutes, my mind wanders right back to my weird sex dream. It was a dream, right? An awkward laugh escapes me. What the hell else could it have been? A projected illusion? Shaking off the thoughts, I redouble my efforts in making the windows sparkle.

The mindless work is exactly what I need. Although, now that I think about it, if it was more challenging my thoughts wouldn't keep drifting back to the sex I had in my sleep.

This is freaky. The mind can play horrible tricks on you. Is it because I've been considering committing to Candy that these buried desires come to the surface? Does it mean maybe I'm questioning my stability with her? If she was the right one for me would I dream about being with them?

Damn, this sure as hell isn't helping. I need to do more complicated stuff than scrubbing and cleaning and stocking stuff.

"Okay, man." I call out while returning the supplies to their place. "I'm done. What's next? Can I fuel it up?"

"We don't fuel up in here. We tow the copter out to where the fuel is."

"Yeah, that makes sense," I say, shaking my head. "Sorry, guess I'm still waking up. What else can I do?"

"Um... let me see... I wasn't expecting any help. I've been working since the orders came down to get the helicopter ready. But an extra set of hands is always good. Let me finish up under the hood and then we can tow the bird out. Why don't you go get the truck with the hitch on it?"

"Sure," I reply. Before I go to do as he asked, another thought occurs to me. "Diego, you worked on the plane before they left, right? Did you see anything funny?"

He leans back out from the engine compartment. "What do you mean by funny? The plane didn't need any work, it was routine maintenance and systems check before they went up." His face goes from relaxed and inquisitive to sharp and offended in the span of a few sentences. "Jon, are you suggesting maybe I missed something?"

"No, I wasn't trying to suggest you did anything. More like wondering what could have happened to the plane and why it went down."

Diego's heated tone matches his expression. "Don't you think I've been racking my brain with the same questions? Did I miss something, did I forget an item on the checklist? Not that I could when I got the damn clipboard right there when I'm going through the systems check. Honestly," he shakes his head and scratches behind his ear. "I have no idea what the hell could've happened. I'm hoping when we get to the wreckage, we can take a looksee."

A fter we get the copter fueled up, Diego suggests we take it up for a test flight before heading out on the search, just in case we need to tweak anything or a light needs replacing. I climb in the back and buckle in, only to be jolted a moment later when Candy knocks on the window.

I holler up to Diego to wait and throw open the sliding door. "Hey, what are you doing here?"

"I got your note. Thought I'd come by and help."

"We're done, but thanks. Going up for a short test flight before we leave on the search. I'll be back soon."

"I can help the search. Kind of like last time, remember when you needed help finding the hunters?"

Frustration fills me. "Yeah, except this time Vivian and Rafe are here. Have you forgotten?"

"No, I haven't forgotten." Her smiling face falters a bit, and she reaches up to twist the silver chain at her neck. "But maybe you did. Didn't we talk about, you know, telling them about us? This seems to be the perfect time. I could help, if you give me the chance. Fly out to scout ahead as an eagle, or an owl. I may not be able to cover as much distance as a helicopter, but my eyesight will be better, and I can get closer to the ground to check for debris."

"I appreciate the offer, hon. But I'm not so sure it's a good idea."

"Why not? You've got one helicopter—it doesn't matter how many eyes are in it, you still only have the one helicopter. Not using me is kind of like not using the only two guns you own when you go into a gunfight, and leaving your shotgun at the house."

Her eyes open wide, their deep brown depths showing honesty and sincerity. She really does think this is a good idea. I know she has to meet them, I swear I'm not acting like some stupid teenager afraid to introduce his girlfriend to his parents, despite what everyone is saying. There is this feeling inside me, I'm not quite sure how to describe it, it's a cross between despair and excitement. It makes me feel like I want to throw up.

"Okay," I say. "Let me think about it, all right? We need to focus on getting the helicopter ready and get out there searching."

Disappointment crosses her features. "I get it Jon, I really do. We've only been together for a few weeks—and you've pledged yourself to a master vampire."

I glance upfront, the tension inside me growing. She talks about this stuff as if everyone knows. Thankfully, Diego's occupied with running through all the switches and testing of things, and he's not paying attention to us. Good.

"Can we talk about this later? I know your heart is in the right place but this is not where we should be discussing it," I raise my eyebrows, and motion to Diego with my head. "You get what I mean, right?"

She rocks back on her heels, clearly annoyed. "Whatever. You're going to be leaving the resort soon. Without me, right? You, Rafe, Vivian—just the three of you." The way she says it has me flash-backing to my recent dream and feeling guilty. "You either tell her now, or you spring it on her after you've left when she's going to feel vulnerable and not her best. Do you really think that's a wise idea?"

I can't deny she's making sense. If I were to put myself in Vivian shoes, where I'm trying to battle, conceivably, what could be the biggest conflict I've ever faced in a half millennia, and my right-hand man is hiding something from me, how would I react to that? Dammit, I hate it when she's right.

"Okay, you've made your point. I do think you'd be an asset during the rescue. And you're right, I should tell them about us sooner rather than later. But, can't you also understand where this puts me? I need to find the right time. I need to find the right words, and so far 'this,'" I motion back and forth between us with my hands, "is bigger than I ever intended. Our relationship has gone on longer than I feel comfortable hiding a secret from her—and she's gonna be looking in my mind later." A sigh eases out of me. "I need to do it. And there's probably no 'right' time."

Candy leans in to rest a hand on my knee, and gently draws me forward for a kiss. Her soft lips brush mine, the lingering warmth calming the conflict racing inside me. Why am I so undecided? Is it fear?

"Don't beat yourself up over this, Jon. You're thinking about it way too much."

Impulsively, I decide to end all this back and forth crap.

"You're right. Let's tell them tonight." Her face lights up and I make another quick decision. "Come on," I move to the side to allow her entry, "it's just a short test flight. Might as well join us."

"Sounds like fun," she says while climbing in, her good mood restored.

I signal to Diego we're ready to take off, and slip on a headset, handing Candy one as well and adjusting them to a closed channel between the two of us. Within minutes we're airborne. Candy can't hide her enthusiasm, she's practically wiggling in her seat. "I'm so excited! I've never flown in a helicopter before."

I motion to her jumpsuit. "Really? I never would have figured. You look the part."

She smiles and unzips the front, revealing she's naked underneath. "I want to help. Thought I could change into a bird and fly down for a closer look if we see anything."

"Um... okay. But that would only work if it's just the two of us."

She motions to Diego, whose attention is not on us. "You think he can see? His eyes are scanning out the windshield. I'll be fine."

Unsure what to say, I sit back in my seat and wait. The door to the helicopter lies open, the wind rushing in to whip our clothes back and forth.

"So tell me," Candy says, "why isn't the local search and rescue on top of things?"

"Because we don't want them to find Drew and the boys."

"I know why we don't want them on the job, but what reasonable excuse did you guys give them to keep them from starting a search?"

"We told them the plane went down, we'd heard from the survivors, and had arranged transport back. And that no medical assistance was needed."

"And just like that, they believed you and called off the search?"

"Well, if you're an ancient vampire with connections, apparently people listen. Even in backwoods Alaska."

Diego flies us over the vast, untouched forest below. The never-ending sun hangs just above the eastern horizon, teasing us with its glow. It's pre-dawn, despite the light, and I'm tired. I'd like nothing more than to climb back in bed and sleep for a few more hours.

Thinking of my bed brings a combination of elation and guilt. Elation, because I've finally found someone to share my bed on a daily basis, and quite possibly for the foreseeable future. Guilt, not only because of my recent erotic dream, but because Eric and Pat aren't home safely in their beds.

I should probably feel bad for Drew, but oddly, I don't. Maybe it's because the blood sucking fool has already lived for over a century, or it could be because I have a dark suspicion the damned undead bastard would be fine, and it'll be my packmates who are drained of their lives before he meets his maker. Sneaky son of a bitch.

"Thinking about Eric and Pat again?" Candy asks, breaking into my silent musings.

"Yeah, you caught me."

"I'm sure they'll be okay."

"Really?" I snap. "And how can you be so sure? There is one thing I am positive of—and it's that fanged bastard will make sure he's okay before anyone else."

Surprise flits across Candy's face. "I thought he was part of your seethe. You sound kind of pissed."

I shake my head and look out over the blanket of green trees below us. "I'm loyal to Vivian, Rafe, and my pack first, then whomever Vivian has added to her vampire family."

She looks contemplative. "Is that something you three worked out when Eric and Pat arrived?"

"Not verbally, no." Tension coils in my gut. "More implied. Vivian wants me to have my own pack, my own life. She never wanted me to become obsessed with her and lose my sense of self."

Now it's Candy's turn to look out over the vast expanse of Alaska unfolding below us, her expression closed and contemplative. "You're a lucky man, Jon. She's a good woman."

I reach out and take her hand in mine. "So are you. I'm sorry I made you— us—wait to tell them. Not sure if it's my own insecurities or what."

She squeezes my hand. "I understand. Trust me."

"You've made comments before like that. How do you know so much about living with a master vampire?"

"Because I lived with one, too."

Before I have a chance to ask her more about her statement, Diego's voice crackles over our headsets. "We're about ten miles out from the resort. Wanted to give you the heads up in case... you know."

That's his way of referring to whatever 'magic' I hope to achieve with sticking my head out the door, like a damn dog scenting danger, or a tunafish sandwich, on the horizon.

Candy looks at me and smiles, sliding her headset off. "That's my cue, big guy. I want to show you how I can help." She unzips her mechanic's jumpsuit and steps out. In an instant she transforms, the change happening so fast, it's like water pours over her, a new winged shape emerging as the transformation flows across her body.

A very large bald eagle stands in her place, claws curled in the pile of recently discarded clothing and shoes, sharp gaze trained in my direction.

Admiration squeezes the air out of my lungs. "Incredible."

She doesn't respond, stepping carefully out of the pile of clothes before walking awkwardly toward the open door. Without a backward glance, she dives out of the helicopter, head first, wings unfurling the moment she clears the door.

I lean out, fist wrapped around a sturdy hand hold, watching her rapid descent into the vast sky. After watching her for a few minutes, she travels under the copter, out of my sight. I tap the mic button on my headset. "Diego, circle to the left. Let's head back."

The helicopter banks hard, shifting the contents tied down in the cabin of the military-like vehicle. Grabbing a pair of binoculars, I scan the wooded treetops, hoping for a sign of Candy.

She's larger than an average eagle, and stunning in her flight. I know she'd be an asset during the search, but I really wish I didn't have to handle this situation right now, when I'd rather be focused on the rescue.

Life is so much easier without adding love to the mix. Too bad it's also a lot more lonely, too.

CHAPTER SEVENTEEN: ERIC

W e've been slowly making our way northeast with the understanding that eventually we're going to come across Haul Road, the only maintained road that lies between the resort and Fairbanks. Following it will eventually lead us to Coldfoot, which is still farther south than Deadfoot, the village that lies closest to the inn. I laughed the first time I heard the name Coldfoot, but now, as I stumble under the weight of a weak and exhausted vampire, I understand it a bit more.

People who were traveling from Fairbanks to Dead Horse in Purdhoe Bay, which more than likely would have been for the oil industry, would often get 'cold feet' half way there and turn back to Fairbanks. That's how the little town—which is really a last chance stop for gas, hot food, and a bed—found its name.

The ten residents who make up the town often share a chuckle over the visitors who turn back, but they're nice enough to wait until the runners are out of ear shot first.

"Slow down," Drew says, his voice panting. "The sun is too much. I need a break."

Pat stiffens, tension radiating from the grip he has on Drew's midsection. I imagine he's refraining from barking out, "Another one?!?" Which I'm grateful he's able to hold back, because it sure as hell won't help the situation.

We stop near a tall tree, angling Drew's body so he'll get the maximum shade from the sparse leaf coverage.

The battered vampire peers at us through the arm holes of a Victoria's Secret pink tank top tied around his head with paracord. If he wasn't so sorry looking, hunched over and bleeding from the small sections of skin that were exposed during shifts of the fabric, then it'd probably be funny. But as the crotchety old bastard said when Pat first chuckled at his ensemble, "It beats being dead."

The vampire lets out a deep sigh, leaning against the trunk and lowering his head. "I need..."

"Let me guess," Pat says. "More blood? If we keep feeding you, we may become too weak to continue carrying you."

He laughs, a raspy sound. "Weak werewolves? Now there's a thought."

"He's right," I say. "We're not regular soldiers anymore, Pat. We can handle this." I step closer, lifting my wrist to Drew. "Here, man. If you need it, I'm here."

The cowering vampire lifts the tank above his chin and I place my skin against his lips. Drew's weakness is so severe he can barely use a sharp fang to pierce the flesh and drink. Or, I could be wrong, and he's holding back his inner hunger to ensure he doesn't attempt to drink me down in one gulp.

Pat looks on, his lip curled in disgust or annoyance, I can't tell which. I hope he'll eventually understand. It shouldn't matter that Drew's not pack, not a werewolf, and technically no longer human. Being humane in our actions toward him defines *us* more than it's a reflection of him being a blood-sucking parasite.

My old friend appears to have contained his inner conflicts for now, and works to rearrange the clothing covering Drew's hands, cringing at the blood dripping from a burn on his pinkie finger. "I'll donate next time, Drew. Just let us know when you need it. I won't be shitty about it, I promise."

Finally eager to do something useful, rather than complain, he takes off the backpack snagged from the wreckage and pulls out two water bottles. He twists off the top and hands a bottle to me. "Drink it, man. We've got a long walk ahead of us. You'll be able to produce more blood as you walk if you stay hydrated."

Next, he fishes back into the bag and pulls out a protein bar. "Eat this next, to make sure you don't get dizzy from blood loss."

I set down my water bottle and grab the offered food. "Thanks."

Drew pulls back, his mouth utterly clean, as is my wrist. "No, thank *you*. Thank you both. I wouldn't be able to go on if it wasn't for the two of you."

Happy he recognizes what we're doing for him, I try to add some levity to the situation. "Hey, all of a sudden living above the Arctic circle in summer doesn't seem like such a good idea, does it?"

"Ha!" Drew barks out, the sound forced from his lungs. "The understatement of the year, right there. If I'd thought the plane would go down, I never would have volunteered to teach you bastards how to fly in the summer."

Pat eases his shoulder under Drew's arm, helping to shift the thinner man's weight back onto his broader shoulders. "Yeah, well, who the hell ever counts on the plane going down? That was fucking freaky."

Even though Drew's been giving us flight lessons for a few months now, I don't know enough about the mechanics of a plane to harbor a guess as to why our aircraft stopped working mid-flight. Without thinking, the first thing that comes to mind pops out of my mouth, "Hey—here's a thought. Could it have been sabotage?"

Drew staggers and I slip his other arm over my shoulders. "I don't know," he says. "Anything is possible. I'm sure we'd need experts to examine the wreckage to determine."

Pat shakes his head. "Nah, not gonna happen. Who the hell would travel back there to check? I don't think it was sabotage. There's no one on the resort who'd wish us harm." After a few moments of silence, Pat asks, "What about that chick in the dining room you were hitting on last week?"

"Come on, man. I asked her out on a date. That's not a I-must-kill-them-in-a-fiery-plane-crash worthy event."

Undeterred by his physical pain, Drew whispers, "What... about... you, Pat? Who'd you bang and piss off?"

"That is so unfair, man. And besides, you're just guessing on the pissed-off part. The ladies I'm with aren't complaining in the end."

I bark out a laugh. "Is that because they're mute or asleep?"

"Snaggle-toothed bastard! Shut the hell up. I'd never touch a girl who was passed out. Give me some credit, man. Well, except maybe to snuggle up next to her and sleep off my own hangover."

I look ahead, through the bush, wondering if we're heading in the right direction. Being this far north also means you can't use the sun as a guide and your magnetic compass may screw up, too.

"Does anyone know where we're going?" I ask, starting to worry as the day seems to drag on forever. Okay, that's a valid reason to not be so happy about the constant daylight. It's hard to gauge how long you've been doing something, especially if you're lost in thought or struggling to make your way through woods that have probably never seen a human before.

"I have a vague idea," Pat answers.

"Should we be worried?"

"I...ah" Drew stammers. "I know where we are. Or more importantly, I know exactly where Vivian is."

"Really? Where is she now?"

"That way," he says, pointing straight to the left of us.

"How does that work?"

"We're linked. Through blood. I can sense her in my mind, deep down in a corner, like her presence, or a connection, always lingers. She never pushes her way into my mind like I imagine most manipulators would do if they could. Considering all she can do, she's pretty respectful."

We're all quiet for a moment while his words sink in.

"That's creepy as fuck," Pat says. "How the hell do you sleep? Jeez, or do the horizontal mambo with Chelly? Aren't you afraid you'll have an extra set of eyes on you... you know... while you're getting busy?"

"Do you actually review the words you want to speak," Drew's voice pants out in bursts while trying to step over a large fallen branch, "*before* they make it out of your mouth?"

I laugh and we drift into silence, walking companionably at a slow and steady pace.

W e've been walking for hours. I glance at my watch, worried. The plane went down around eight last night and now it's close to seven in the morning. Drew has been steadily slowing down for the past hour or so, and I know exactly what that means.

"Drew? Are you okay, man?" I ask, puncturing his almost trance-like state of self-control. "You've been awfully quiet lately."

"Yeah, I'm okay. Don't worry about me."

Pat's labored breathing sounds from my right. "How long have we been walking? How far do you think we've come? Oh, wait—more importantly, how far do we still have to go?"

"We've been walking for about nine hours at a slow to moderate pace, well, at least for werewolves and vamps. If we've covered more than two and half to three miles per hour I'd be surprised."

"Shit. Considering how far away we are, we're going to be walking for a really long time. Without much in the way of food or water—plus, we're caring for a hungry, injured vampire. Dude, this is a recipe for disaster."

Concentrating on putting one foot in front of the other, my reply is terse. "We've already covered this. Staying at the crash site wasn't an option. How would we have explained Drew's aversion to the sun? Or his fangs when he vamped out from hunger?"

"Yeah, but won't the searchers expand their rescue

attempts further? Seems like we'll be letting a lot of people waste their time and man hours."

My normally calm demeanor cracks under the strain to keep moving. "You're worried about the rescue workers? What the fuck do you care? It's not like we can change what the rescuers would do. We can't exactly call them up on the phone."

Pat's snarky expression turns sour, and he stumbles a bit. "Who got your panties in a bunch? Geez. I was just wondering."

Taking a deep breath, I try to calm my whip-lash moods. I'm exhausted and strung out, just like him, but I've got to hold it together for all of us. "If we keep going due east, we're bound to hit Haul Road eventually."

Pat's frustration is almost palpable. "And then what? We flag down a passing trucker and hope they'll stop? This is asinine."

"Do you have a better suggestion?" I ask, my annoyance getting the better of me again. "I'm all ears, fucktard."

Before Pat can respond, Drew whispers, "Vivian will come."

"What was that?" Pat asks, leaning closer to our battered friend.

"He said Vivian would come for us."

"How can he be so sure? Why wouldn't she send someone else?"

The ragged vampire pants out, "Because she can sense us with her mind. We are her seethe. She will not abandon us. It is her job as our master."

"We've sworn no loyalty to her, Drew," Pat responds. "Just

to Jon, as our alpha. She'll have to do her tracking through you, fanger."

Drew smiles, the expression fierce as we slog through the wooded terrain, sheer determination keeping him upright in the growing heat and oppressive sunlight. "You are wrong, young padawan."

"What?" Pat asks.

"You drink the water. On the resort. Vivian runs through your veins."

"What the fuck are you talking about?" demands Pat.

He shakes his head, unwilling to waste more strength on explaining something we've been too blind to pay attention to. "You'll see."

Pat jostles him, perhaps on purpose to get more out of the tired man, but Drew ignores him, concentrating on putting one foot in front of the other.

"He makes a good point," I say after a few dozen yards. "When we make it to the road, that will be the logical place for them to look for us. Assuming they know we're not dead."

"She'd know we're not dead if she's connected to Drew's mind. So we got that going for us. What did he mean about the water and Vivian?"

I shrug, the movement subtle due to supporting Drew under his arms. "I'm not sure. But if it helps them find us before Drew's survival instinct takes over, then I'm all for it."

Pat stumbles, but doesn't lose his footing, his support on Drew's right side staying true. "Now why did you have to go ahead and say that? Like I need to think about our friend here deciding we're just too delectable and he can't wait any longer?"

Humor bubbles up inside the injured vampire, and he

repeats part of a phrase from our meeting in the basement a lifetime ago. "I prefer pussy—especially over dogs."

A fter another hour, Drew's feet begin to drag. No way to avoid it. He needs more blood.

And it's Pat's turn to donate.

"I need a break," I announce. "Do we have any water or food left?"

We stop, leaning Drew against a tree like last time, and Pat slips the backpack off his shoulders, easing it and himself to the ground. "Yeah. Three more bottles of water and a handful of protein and granola bars. Which do you want?"

My gaze sweeps toward Drew, concern marring my forehead. "How're you doing, old man? Do you need more blood?"

The vampire tries to smile, his cracked, dry lips curving up the barest amount. "Old man? Nice. I think I can manage another couple miles."

"*Manage?* Is that what this is?" Pat straightens, steeling his spine as he stands, and offers his wrist. "If you go any slower, we'll be dragging your skinny ass through these woods. Come on, man. Drink. Get it over with."

Fear slithers across his face, quickly hidden as Drew's cool lips touch his skin. The vampire opens his mouth, and one sharp canine pricks the surface. My oldest friend looks like he's drawing on every ounce of courage he possesses not to pull back and rip his arm away from the weak predator.

Pat closes his eyes, perhaps unwilling to watch the needy undead drink from him. After a moment, his facial expression eases, as if he's relieved there's no pain. Without warning, Drew draws back.

"That's it?" Pat asks. "That wasn't so bad. It didn't even hurt," he says, looking down at his unbroken skin. "You healed the wound already?"

Drew's eyes glaze over and he falls face first to the ground. A low moan escapes his prone form.

"That can't be good," I say while bending down to examine the man. After a moment, I glance up at Pat's wrist. "You dolt. He didn't bite you at all. And now I'm not sure if he can."

"Great. Just great. Are we expected to slice our wrists and literally bleed for the man?"

I reach into my pocket and draw out a folded knife. "Got a better idea?"

Pat takes the offered blade and grimaces. "No. Dammit."

CHAPTER EIGHTEEN: RAFE

The next morning dawns crisp and clear. Despite it being summer, it's often cold in the morning. I don't mind it one bit. Reminds me of springtime in Germany, where I grew up.

Justin sees me pull in to the apartment parking lot and saunters over to the jeep.

"Did you leave the tracking charm for Vivian?" I ask.

"Yup. Gave it to her myself a few minutes ago."

"Great. Thanks."

Concern crosses Justin's face, quickly squashed.

"Don't worry." I say as he reaches for the door handle. "He's tough. He'll be okay.

He hesitates, leaning in the open window. "How did— never mind. How can you be sure?"

"Faith. My wife has a connection with Drew. She'd know if something major happened to any of them."

"Is that why you're not worried?"

I nod as he steps back and opens the door. "Yup. They

might be hurt. They will be dirty and tired. But they will be alive. I can feel it."

He climbs in and we head on our way. After spending all day in his presence, I think I understand more that he likes the quiet spaces Alaska has to offer. He doesn't seem to feel the need to fill in quiet with conversation, so I leave him be to reflect on my own thoughts.

I need to learn magic. I need to be able to protect those I love. No longer do I want my wife to be responsible for more than she already is. I drove her to accept more people, I backed her into situations where I knew the result would be greater numbers in our seethe, and I manipulated events to make it happen. How can I sit back and expect her to be the sole protector of all that we hold dear? I won't.

"Do you have the map?" Justin asks.

"It's near your feet."

He reaches for the paper, unfolding it in his lap. "We've still got a ways to cover. Are you determined to get the whole thing done today? I want to help with the rescue search."

"Justin, I appreciate your concern for your brother. But you do understand the urgency of our situation, right?"

"I think I do. Is there more going on than you guys have led me to believe?"

"You mean more than a group of manipulator vampires ready to wipe us out if we don't join their cause? No. I wouldn't say we purposely led you to believe one thing over another. It was more about how much, for your own safety, did you need to know."

Deciding that's not enough, I try explaining it another way. "Even though Jon, Vivian, and I will be leaving soon, we're leaving behind everything we hold dear. This perimeter ward is vitally important to the safety of the resort's inhabitants. Your help in securing the ward around the property will go a long way in easing our minds when we're gone."

"Have you thought about the fact that we're tuning the wards to you and Vivian, and yet you won't be here if they get triggered?"

"Yes, I know. The same thought has plagued me. Any suggestions on how we should handle notifications when we're not here? Will you feel the ward being triggered?"

"I will at first, maybe for a few weeks after it's completed. But without my blood fueling it, my connection will fade in time." He sits in quiet for a moment, then says, "Hey, I remember seeing cameras on trees, the ones you mentioned were installed this past spring. How hard would it be to install cameras throughout all the property? I mean, if you and Vivian aren't here for the blood wards to notify you, wouldn't regular technology be the best way to go? It might be a good alternative option."

I turn onto a dirt road, leaving the last of the maintained roads of the resort behind us. "Here's the thing: electricity can be taken out. In the past, our generators have been attacked by enemies. We've done our best to resolve the issue with back-up systems, but losing power is still a weakness that will cripple us. If you rely solely on technology, your enemies can easily foil your security measures with well-placed bombs. If we have magic and technology working hand-in-hand, our hope is there's a higher chance of creating a more secure border."

Justin laughs and shakes his head. "How funny is it, I was just thinking about the recent election. All that talk about border control?"

"Yeah, the United States has nothing on the security of our inn."

After a few minutes of traveling slowly on the dirt road, we stop. Today, we're covering the last forty percent of the perimeter, roughly six miles. I hustle out, new-found strength from the blood exchange pulsing through my veins, pushing me to do more, to move faster, to protect those I love.

Justin exits the cart and grabs his duffle bag. "How comfortable are you with the ritual for the warding spell? Feel like starting today?"

A smile crosses my face and I pat the small vial of my blood I drew this morning. "I'm feeling unstoppable. Let's finish this bitch."

"Good! Glad to hear it. Before you begin, let's practice the fire spell. You were able to get it a couple of times yesterday near the end, so I'd like to run through it again to be sure you can call it forth when needed."

We spend twenty minutes going through the hand motions and phrasing he taught me, and several times I'm able to call forth a small spark to ignite the tinder set out. It's still not consistent yet, but hopefully after performing the rituals over and over today for each ward we set, I'll have it down pat.

We work in silence for the next hour or so, speaking only when Justin feels the need to correct my phrasing or adjust the spell ingredients I've assembled. I like the slow and steady pace, it appeals to the methodical part of me that keeps me disciplined on a day to day basis.

Like going to the gym. I may not enjoy it, but once the habit is ingrained, I don't feel good when I skip a session.

After a few hours, we're finally done. I expected to experience a tingling of some kind when the wards were all connected, but instead, I feel an angry buzzing against my senses. It's uncomfortable and triggers a need to scratch a spot between my shoulder blades.

"Uh-oh," Justin says, his eyes filling with alarm.

"Crap, did we do something wrong?"

"No. On the contrary. We did it exactly right."

"Then why do you look concerned?"

"Because the sensation your feeling? Like there's a target on your back covered in itching powder?"

"Yeah?"

"That's what it feels like when the ward is triggered."

"I don't understand."

"Rafe, it means danger is already here. On the resort."

"Shit." I grab my phone to text Dria, only to see that her and Jon left two minutes ago to search for the boys.

CHAPTER NINETEEN: JON

After we've been in the air for a while, I notice the bird. It's flying below us, but definitely going in our direction and flying much faster than a bird that size should be able. As it comes closer, I get a better look at it. Dammit, it's a bald eagle. I know Candy wants to help, but I'd really hoped Vivian and I could sneak off without her being aware. No such luck.

I steal a glance at Vivian, who insisted on coming, stating she had experience with Justin's tracking charms and could locate them faster in conjunction with her blood connection with Drew. We're both sitting in the back of the helicopter looking out the windows and that's when I notice Vivian has spotted the eagle too.

Her cool voice sounds through my headphones, "There's something odd about that bird. Almost like it's following us."

Guilt, panic, and impulsiveness all vie for attention in my brain at once. I've got to come clean. There will never be a perfect time, but what's more important is that I stop lying to the person I'm loyal to.

"Uh... I've got something to tell you, Vivian." I turn to face her, where she's buckled into the seat next to me.

Her right eyebrow rises, a curious look on her face. "Do you now? I wondered when you'd finally be ready to talk to me. Go ahead."

"That eagle down there? That's my girlfriend. Her name is Candy. I'm sorry didn't tell you sooner. I wasn't sure what to say, how to say it, or even if I should. But I knew I would eventually have to."

Vivian's gaze sharpens as she looks out the window and then back to me. "Is she a magic user? Is she using a spell to make her an eagle? I wasn't aware that there were were-eagles."

My heart thuds in my chest, part of me wants to throw up, I'm so nervous. But this is going better than expected so far—she hasn't lashed out in rage—things could always be worse. "No, she's a shifter. She can change shape into just about anything she sees or has a picture of."

"Really?" Both eyebrows creep up her forehead in fascination. "Now that could be interesting. How did you two meet?"

Is it my imagination or is there a twinkle in her eye when she asks? "She uh... She was a member of Romeo's pack. They were here during the big game hunt."

"Hmm..." she says while tapping a finger on her lips. "I don't recall there being a Candy on the list from Romeo. Was she a last-minute addition?"

And now this is when things are going to get really awkward. "She was on the list all right, but under another name. Spike."

Vivian's gaze sharpens again, her eyebrows rising once

more. "Am I to understand she was here as a *he?* Surely you must not have known when you first met her as a him, right?"

"You're right. I didn't know who he was at the time. But there was something between us. Even when she was a guy. I... I thought I was going crazy for a while there. You know, like I liked guys all of a sudden or something." I shake my head and look down at my feet.

Vivian reaches a hand over and pats me on the thigh. "Don't be so hard on yourself, Jon. Attraction knows no gender boundaries. Attraction is chemistry, pure and simple. So what do you think—I take it things are going well? After all, that was weeks ago. Have you been together all this time?"

I look at her hand covering mine, and then glance up to see her smiling eyes, almost like they're laughing at me. "You've known, haven't you? You've known all this time. And to think I was afraid to tell you. I've been sweating bullets about this for weeks on what to say and how to approach you. And... And you really don't mind, do you?"

"Oh, Jon, all I've ever wanted is for you to find happiness— to be truly happy. For you, that state will never be achieved with Rafe and me. Deep down, what you desire above all else, what you crave with every fiber of your being, is to have your own pack, and that means a packmate. And no matter how close the three of us will be, that is something we can never be for you."

"Rafe knows, too?"

"Of course. I think he may have seen her the other day. He mentioned something. But I didn't want to press for details. I knew you would come to us when you were ready, when you felt comfortable enough to say something. What took you so long?"

I shrug my shoulders. "I dunno. I was scared. It's stupid now that I think about it. Maybe a part deep inside me really just needed to be sure, you know?"

She nods in understanding. "Is she the one? The one who will be your mate?"

Happiness surges inside me at her question. "I hope so. But I knew I couldn't make that decision until you and Rafe were a part of it."

"Did you really expect us to meet her and give you our stamp of approval? Honestly, I wanted to stay as far out of it as I possibly could. So that we didn't influence your decision at all. This needs to be something you do for *you*."

A silence stretches between us as I contemplate her words, the only sound the beating helicopter blades above us.

"Is that all that she really needs to be—'the right one' for me? What if you like her and Rafe hates her? What if she refuses to bond with you? What happens then?"

She smiles reassuringly, and pats my thigh once more before removing her hand. "There are some things no one can refuse. But that's neither here nor there. More importantly, she needs to get to know us, to decide if she wants to be a part of what we share. That will take time." She looks out the window, her eyes tracking the eagle. "I look forward to meeting her."

The panic I felt before grips my heart again. "Umm.... Well, uh... you kind of have met her already."

Vivian rips her gaze from the window and says, "And how's that?"

Unable to meet her penetrating stare, I look away. "Mariposa."

Vivian laughs. "Clever bitch. Very clever. She came in

under my radar to get to know me. Smart girl you've got there, Jon."

This feels surreal. It's not bad, like I feared. Rafe knew. It seems like the only one to worry about has been me. I was the problem all along. And why is that? God, this is a big step. Have I known Candy long enough? I can't believe I've been practically frozen with indecision about this.

Love should be easy. And I made everything harder than it needed to be. "I'm confused. This mean you're not angry?"

"What did you expect of me, Jon? Did you think I fly off the handle, and try to scare off your girlfriend? Or, I don't know, maybe look inside her head to make sure she had the best intentions toward you? Were you worried that Rafe and I would somehow not approve?" A smirk forms on her face.

I know she's teasing me but the shock bubbling inside doesn't quite know what to do with this new development.

"So... Let me get this straight. You're not worried about who I'm dating, and you *don't* want to look in her head?"

She reaches out once again to pat my knee reassuringly before drawing her hand away. "Oh, Jon, poor misguided, Jon." She laughs again. This time loud and long. "Love is what I've always dreamed of for you."

My eyebrows creep up my forehead. She's dreamed of me finding a mate? It's something I've dreamed about but why would she? My mind skitters back to the dream I experienced last night, and with it comes confusion. What does the couple want from me? If last night's dream truly was a shared experience like I think it was, which one of them had the dream? I know it sure as hell wasn't me.

"Jon, no matter what you think of me and Rafe and the relationship the three of us share, it will always be *our* relationship. You know you are invaluable to us—we need you in our lives. There's no one we trust by our side, and frankly *with* our lives, except you. But what does that mean for you? When do *you* get to have the love of your life? When do *you* get to start a family, when do *you* get to *live?*"

She shakes her head, looks back out the window, leaning forward a bit to see if she can spot the eagle. "Whether you believe it or not, I've always had your best interests at heart. Pledging your loyalty to me and becoming a vampire servant was never meant to be a prison sentence. You've never experienced true happiness of your own. Working with us is not a full-time job, right?" She turns and looks at me, her questioning expression indicating this time I'm supposed to answer.

"No, you're right. It's not a full-time job. And I do need those things you mentioned. A love of my own, a family. I... I... I guess, I'm just in shock. I expected..."

"You expected me to go bat shit crazy on your ass, right? Come on, Jon, we've been friends for almost eight years now. Eight. Years. Don't you deserve to take a mate by now?"

I stare at her across the space between us and I don't have an answer. Was it all my own internal fears and self-doubts, and I projected all of it onto Vivian? As if she would be the one to make my life a living hell, or ruin my relationship? God forbid I actually take responsibility for my own life and relationships—and whether either works or not is totally my fault.

"Okay, so you're all right with this? And so is Rafe?"

"Trust me, Jon. This is something we've both wanted for you for a very long time. I will do everything in my power to not scare away your intended."

"Whoa, hold on now. I don't know if *intended* is the right word." My brow furrows. "But if I'm thinking about her as a mate, then I guess 'intended' is as good as any, right?"

"How about we talk about this more when we're on the ground—and after we've found our missing friends." She holds the charm. "It's getting warm. The same thing it did when we went in the right direction while hunting Rolando in Buenos Aires. We're not only traveling in the right direction, but I think we're getting closer."

"Okay, we'll talk later. But don't think this is the end of it. I want you to meet her, I just wasn't sure when the time was right."

"Yeah, yeah. I'm looking forward to meeting her. I'm bummed I won't have a dog but, I can get another one." And with that she taps a button on her mic, opening the channel to Diego for him to hear us as well. "Do you see the eagle behind us?"

There's a crackle of static before he responds, and he says, "Yeah, I see it. Are you worried about me hurting it or something?"

"No. I want you to slow down and follow it." And with that she looks over at me and winks. "You said she wants to help, right?" I nod. "She knows what we're looking for. It's a plane crash site. She's got better eyes than we do. To find a needle in a haystack, she's the one to follow."

Hope surges within me, battling at the same time my own inner demons. Was I the cause of all my drama? And if I am, what does that say about me? If I look deep inside myself, would I have seen their acceptance sooner?

And if I would have, then what does it truly mean—that perhaps instead, what I've been doing is more about me.

How I feel about Candy. Whether or not I'm ready to commit.

We watch my girlfriend fly in circles, hovering steady above her, before she picks up speed and goes in another direction. We fly in silence for about twenty minutes. The energy in the cabin spikes as we fly toward Fairbanks, which can only mean one thing. We're finally getting closer to the crash site.

As the time progresses, Vivian presses her face closer to the window, she's literally watching the eagle like a hawk. I smile. I can't believe this is going to go better than I expected. Granted, we're currently running a rescue mission to recover our missing seethe and packmates—but other than that, things are good.

After all, Vivian's connection to Drew would indicate if he was truly in danger or dead, right? And if he's dead, then more than likely so are Eric and Pat. So, since we haven't heard different from Vivian, I'm assuming the best. That all three are alive and well—just waiting for us to find them.

"Down there!" Vivian calls out. "I see something. It could be a lot of garbage... I'm not sure. Let's go for a closer luck."

Diego's voice responds over the headphones, "Yes, ma'am. I see an area along a stream bed I can set the chopper down. If this is the crash site, that's gotta be where they tried to take the plane down. Give me a few minutes to land."

To his word, after finding a suitable place, the bird's landing gear connects with the dry stream bed. He shuts off the blades and gives us the okay to disembark. Candy is nowhere in sight as we slide the doors back and jump out.

Vivian gathers her long hair in one hand at the nape of her neck and dashes for the trees. I follow, turning and giving a thumbs up to Diego and then hold up my hand with five fingers to indicate we'll be back in five minutes. He nods and I turn back to follow Viv.

She's on a mission, there's no doubt about it. She calls out, already racing ahead of me, "The wreckage is here!" We run together, then skid to a stop in a larger clearing around the dry bed, about another two hundred yards downstream. The sight stills my heart. Twisted metal, burnt dashboard, pieces of the wing and cabin strewn about the clearing. A bloody front seat, the seatbelt dangling, also dark with blood. How the hell did they walk away from this?

Vivian answers the question she heard my head, "They survived because they're supernatural. There's no way in hell anyone else could have walked away from this."

The whole prop plane is in pieces, strewn up and down the shoreline. Wings torn off among the trees, the back end of the plane almost looking like it exploded with packages.

Within a minute, we find a seat completely by itself torn apart from the hull of the plane. I bend closer, taking a deep breath. "It's Eric. I know the smell of his blood."

"Well, that's awfully handy."

Candy, having located the site first, circles above us and lands on a nearby tree branch.

Vivian waves to her. "Hello, Candy. Jon and I had a nice talk in the helicopter." The vampire dips her head regally. "I can't wait until we get a chance to meet—in person this time."

Candy starts to transform, and once again I feel as if there's a vise around my heart. Am I ready for this? For my two worlds to collide? But to my surprise, my girlfriend doesn't shift into her human form. She shifts into a black and tan bloodhound. Of course! Why didn't I think that?

The bloodhound races over to the seat with the blood and takes a great big whiff. A loud booming bark fills the clearing as the bloodhound's tail wags.

Vivian smiles, a crooked, cocky grin if I ever saw one. "Now that's a smart bitch you've got there, Jon."

Candy the bloodhound walks around and heads toward a tree set off from the stream. She barks again and we join her. It looks as if the three of them sat here for a while in the shade.

"Yes, I believe you're right," Vivian says, as if she understood exactly what the bark meant. "I'm smelling vampire blood. Which means Drew has been injured as well."

"But he can heal quickly. Do we need to be concerned?"

Vivian looks at the sun high overhead, shielding her eyes. "He's not as old as I am. He won't be able to handle the sun for long, especially with wounds and blood loss. I'm sure the boys will help him. But for how long they safely can is what I worry about most."

"Candy got the right idea to track them as a bloodhound. By the scent, they've left here hours ago. I'd like to change into my wolf form so we can track them together. How about we use the mental connection you and I share while you fly with Diego and direct him to follow?"

"That'll work. I like the idea."

"Great. You take my clothes."

Unwilling to strip in front of Vivian with my girlfriend watching, I decide to go behind a tree. Call me a wimp if you want, but avoiding conflict is much safer.

I take my clothes off and fold them, calling the transformation as quickly I can. Not literally between one blink of an eye and the next, but certainly much faster than most Weres. I emerge from behind the tree, my tail held high, with the clothes in my mouth, and the relief of happiness seeping through me. We're almost there. We're going to find them and all will be good.

Candy bounds over to me, her deeper bark more piercing and somehow soul-wrenching then when she was a Pit Bull. She trots over to their scent trail leading off into the woods and I follow, not bothering to look back because I trust Vivian will follow us in the chopper with Diego.

That's what you do. You trust the people who have your back. With strong support, you can accomplish anything. Even if it's as simple as tracking a blood trail through the woods.

CHAPTER TWENTY: ERIC

The sun blazes overhead, flashes of its warmth penetrating my skin whenever we step from beneath the shade of the trees above us. I don't mind the heat, but for the vampire supported between myself and my best friend Pat, the rays of the sun don't bring just heat, but a burning blistered skin, red with pain. My muscles ache, my body stinks, and I feel weaker than a two-week old kitten drenched in water.

Drew's step fumbles, his weight pulling across my shoulders, causing me to grasp him firmer under the arm and brace with my legs, so we don't all go down in a sprawling heap on the forest floor.

"How much further to Haul Road, do you think?" Pat asks.

"Don't you think if I knew that I would have said something by now?" Frustration and exhaustion make me sharper than normal. "I mean seriously dude, if I had a clue I would have said something a few hours ago."

"No need to get testy with me, you snaggle-toothed

bastard. I was just wondering. Or maybe 'hoping' would be a better word."

A sigh escapes me. "I don't mean to sound like a son of a bitch, sorry."

"Stop," Drew's voice whispers. "I need to stop for the night."

"Night? This isn't night, man," Pat says. "I think the sunlight is making him loopy. He did say night, right?"

I scan the tree line ahead of us, looking for something, anything, that we can seek shelter under. Up ahead, to the right, is a denser grouping of pines. Their branches cast a dark shadow near the base of their trunks, providing cover.

"Over there," I say, with a nod of my head. Pat's gaze follows the direction I've indicated, and his chin dips in understanding.

"Just a little farther, Drew. Can you handle it?"

In response, Drew's knees collapse, forcing all his weight on us. "Shit," exclaims Pat, "for a dead guy, he sure is heavy."

Seeing no other choice, I shift my weight and turn toward Drew, "Alley—ooop," I say while placing my shoulder in his middle and hoisting him over my shoulder like a sack of potatoes.

Once he's up and I'm steady, I head toward the trees.

"Come on, man. You got to face the facts," Pat says, pointing at our ever-weakening friend. "He's not going to make it. Dude, are you listening to me? How far is Fairbanks from Deadfoot?"

Unwilling to listen and determined to keep moving, I shake my head, hoping to drive his words away. "Just let it go, man. We have to keep going. And we are not leaving him behind. *Leave no man behind.* Is that something you've forgotten so soon?" I reach the shade and ease our friend's body down carefully, mindful of his many open wounds.

The frustration seeps off Pat, making his face twisted and sour. Reminds me of one time we were drinking in the woods in West Milford. The drunker he got the more belligerent he became with his opinion and being right. But then again, he could be right this time and it's my own stubbornness that's not allowing me to admit it. Dammit. I check on Drew instead.

He lies on his side in the shade, arms draped over his head, unmoving, un-breathing, and by all appearances, he looks dead. Until you look closely and see fresh blood oozing from the new sun sores he's received.

Without warning, Pat shoves me from behind and I stumble forward, catching myself on a branch. "What the fuck, man?"

"Listen to me, you arrogant bastard! We don't know how far we are to Haul Road. We're still easily over a hundred miles from Deadfoot. There is no way we can keep going at this pace. We have no idea when help will arrive." He shoves me again, this time in my chest. "Are you listening? Are you really listening to me now, Eric? We can't save him by ourselves. He's going to lose it. Look at him! Would you look at him!"

Tension and rage tightens my fists. It takes everything in me not to punch him right in the face. I can't believe he wants to leave our friend here. Just leave him in the woods to freaking roast to death. "I hear you. You're shouting. It's kind of difficult not to hear you, fuck face." I cross my arms over my chest. "I'm not leaving him here. It feels wrong."

"We're not deserting him on a freakin' battlefield. We'd be

going for help. Sure as shit beats dragging his weak, bloody ass with us."

Drew moans softly from the ground. Small whispers of "go, go, go" escaping from his bloodied, cracked lips.

"Fine," I say, frustration getting the better of me. "What do you suggest?"

"That we dig a narrow, shallow trench, put him in it, and cover him up so he's protected from the sun."

"How will we lead the others back to him? You know they're looking for us. We could build a signal fire, use green wood so it would be really smoky. Maybe then they would find us?"

"Yeah," Pat agrees. "We could do that. But you're forgetting about search parties from Fairbanks. If they're out looking for us, the fire will lead a clear path to where we are. With a hungry vampire waiting for them."

I look over at Drew's huddled form, guilt seeping through me. "But to just leave him. It's wrong. What about bears and wolves?"

"He's got deadly and dangerous predator written all over him. It's in his blood, his energy, his very scent. Animals aren't stupid. They sense it. I don't think anything is gonna bother him out here."

"Drew?" I ask. "What do you think? Should we leave you, buried safely underground, and go get help?"

"Go, go, go…"

"I think that says it all." Pat says with a smile. "He's on board with the idea. Let's get digging."

Without further ado, Pat and I grab some thick sticks and use their ragged ends to clear the pine needles, leaves, and loose surface dirt from an area underneath the tree. We dig for a few minutes until we have a trench roughly the length of his body, and about a foot to a foot and a half deep.

Pat straightens from his kneeling position, wiping his sweaty face on a sleeve. "I think it's good, don't you? We're not digging a real grave or anything like that, you know." He finishes with a chuckle, perhaps trying to lighten up the situation. I don't know, but it seems weird to be burying our friend.

I nod my agreement, uncomfortable with what we're doing, but understanding we really have no choice if we want to get him help before it's too late. And what exactly is *too late* for an injured vampire?

Pat and I carefully shift, drag, and lift Drew as painlessly as we can to settle him into the trench. Unwilling to put dirt on his open wounds, despite the fact he probably wouldn't get an infection being undead and all, I grab a handful of dried leaves and scatter those over him.

"Go," he rasps. Go..."

"Don't worry, man, we'll be out of here soon. We will bring back help. I promise."

Once I feel we've covered him as best we can, and there's no exposed skin showing, we retreat back into the bright sunlight.

"We'll travel faster as wolves," Pat says while staring up at the sun. "It's only going to get hotter the longer we wait."

"It's not like he's going to melt. He's in the shade, covered up. We've done everything we can."

Pat smirks, a little of the smart ass coming back to the forefront. "I know that, man. It was my fucking awesome idea." He pulls his shirt over his head, tossing it in the direction of the backpack.

I begin to unbutton my shirt, when a snapping twig behind us pulls me around. Drew staggers out from under the tree limbs, leaves stuck to the wet bloodied patches of his exposed blistering skin, shredded fabric hanging from his limbs, his eyes a solid black.

Pat gets out, "What—" before Drew attacks him, leaping at my friend, his mouth wide open, sharp fangs descended and ready to feed.

"No!" Pat stumbles backward as I lunge forward, tackling the slim vampire. "Stop it, Drew! Get control of yourself!"

He's like a rabid beast, gnashing his teeth and growling. His black eyes appear feral and maddened. This creature is not my friend. But my friend lies somewhere deep inside the insanity that currently grips him.

Drew's mouth latches onto the thick muscle between my shoulder and neck, like he's going to tear a hunk of flesh from my body. "Stop it! You can beat this!" I reach up to wrench his head away from me and scream to Pat to help.

Pat bounds up, races over to our position on the ground and punches Drew in the back of the head hard.

"Hit him again!" I yell. "Hit him again!" That first blow loosened his hold on my shoulder, and all I can think of is getting this leech off me before he does permanent damage.

Pat's face scrunches up in pain as his fist flies forward again and again, pummeling the vampire until the man's jaw slackens. As quick as it started, the energy and fight drains out of Drew and his body lies limp against me. I shift my hands to his chest and push him off, strangled gasps of air wheezing from my lungs.

"Holy shit. That was intense. We've got to get the hell out of here before he wakes up." Pat leans over and offers me a hand up. He pulls me to my feet, and I stand, bent over at the waist, hands on my knees breathing hard. I can't believe it. We waited too long.

"Let's drag him back to the trench, cover him up, and run a mile before we shift. I want more space between him and us when we're changing." I stand and stare my friend. "Thanks."

"Damn straight. You'd have done the same for me."

Once we're done, and have tied Drew's hands behind his back, Pat and I take off into the woods, sprinting as fast as we can from the hellish scene. Holy crap, Drew tried to drain us. Deep inside I know it wasn't him. I don't know what it was— and I hope to never have to face such a reaction in Vivian—but whatever happened to him showed in his eyes. They were black, bottomless pits. That creature wasn't the man I've come to know.

After a few minutes, Pat lunges ahead of me, indicating we've gone far enough. We slow, and eventually come to a stop, thoroughly winded from the headlong sprint through the woods.

"I still can't believe that shit just happened," Pat says. "It was so damn fast. Normal Drew one minute—crazy, psycho Drew the next."

"I know, man. We've got to get him help. I never thought I'd be as happy to be in the middle of nowhere as I am right now. If there had been a village or homestead nearby, who the hell knows what he would've done. I'm glad it was us and not someone weaker."

Pat nods, glances around, and finally pulls his head over shirt, deciding this is the best place as any to transform into wolves. Since he's right, I begin to disrobe as well.

"Hey," Pat says, stopping me. "We should change one at a

time, watching over the other during the shift to make sure we're safe."

I dip my chin in agreement and turn back the way we came, watching for Drew. Even though I seriously doubt the hog-tied vampire would be able to catch up to us in the time it takes us to shift, I'm also not willing to take the risk.

Five agonizing minutes later, Pat has changed to wolf form, and lies on the ground panting. Once he's stable, he stands, shakes himself all over, and stares at me, indicating he's ready. Wasting no time, I strip off my clothes, bundle them up as Pat did with his, and change fast as I can, allowing the painful, agonizingly slow shift to transform my body.

Both of us grab the clothing bundles in our mouths, via loops we made of our pant legs, and race in the direction of the road. I hadn't planned on us running the hundred or so miles to the resort, because I doubt either one of us has the energy, so I sincerely hope we're able to find someone who can help us on Haul Road.

A few minutes after we set out, the unmistakable thump-thump-thump of a helicopter's propellers sounds in the distance. This is one time I wish Pat and I had a telepathic connection, like the magical merry trio does back home.

We stop and turn around, racing toward the sound as it fades in the distance, but the copter can't see us in the dense foliage. Pat looks back where we came, then looks forward, before finally looking to me. He's wearing a comical hang-dog expression of "what now?"

I'm not sure what to do, but instinct tells me we need to go back and protect Drew, or more than likely protect the people who might find Drew. It could be a helicopter from home searching for us. That is, if we even have a helicopter.

But if it's rescuers from Fairbanks and they find the wreckage and send people out after us... they'd have dogs to track, right? Within a few hours, they'd find Drew and then where would we be? There's really no choice. We have to go back.

Pat recognizes my decision, a whine escaping him. Both of us are torn on this one. The consequences lay heavy on my mind, and reluctantly I lead us back to do the right thing. Shifting again so soon is going to hurt like a bitch.

CHAPTER TWENTY-ONE: VIVIAN

The tan and black hound, also known as Candy, is easier to spot from the helicopter than Jon. His mottled fur coloring blends in better with the wilderness around, but thanks to our mental connection I'm able to keep track of them as they run through the woods following the boys' scents.

I direct Diego as he flies. He knows we're following a tracking hound and thanks to a little mental nudge from me, he thinks we brought the dogs along in the helicopter with us. While a lot of the employees have a feeling about what's going on, most of them don't know for sure. Or I should say, none of them know for sure about Jon.

The ones who donate blood, they know vampires are real. We've never really had an open conversation with the employees about other supernatural creatures, as in what exists and what doesn't, and in this case, I've always felt ignorance is bliss. For them, ignorance is safer.

Anxiety bubbles inside me as I watch the two run through the woods. The fact that Eric, Pat, and Drew all had enough sense to leave the plane wreckage, knowing standard procedure would be a rescue party sent out from Fairbanks, means they're thinking clearly.

How far did they get? How far into the woods will we need to track?

We travel father than expected, close to fifteen minutes, before I see Jon and Candy come across something in the woods, and their direction seems to divert. Very soon I see two more wolves racing toward them and the tracking charm burns hot in my pocket. But they're alone. There's no sight of Drew with the two wolves.

I reach through my connection and touch on the neuro pathway leading to Drew, something I've done periodically throughout the whole trip. My mind recognizes his essence. He's still alive, but that's all I can tell for now. But the question remains, what have they done with him? Where is Drew?

"Diego, I believe we found them. Do you see a place we can land?"

"Not yet, ma'am. Give me a minute to circle around and locate a clearing."

I watch the four tiny figures through the window, see them change routes again and head in a more easterly direction. Their path indicates they were going toward Haul Road. Smart. If I were them, now knowing where they landed, I probably would've done the same.

Why leave Drew behind? Something major had to have happened for them to leave him. Men in the military don't normally skip out on a comrade.

Diego's voice comes over the line. "There's a flat, rocky outcropping ahead. It's next to the cliff face, meaning we'll have a sheer drop on one side. But the rocky area is quite large, ideal for a make-shift landing pad. Let me set her down there."

"Great. Take us down when you're ready."

While I could've flown the helicopter myself, I don't think I could've managed following Jon and Candy on the ground as easily without Diego. He's a top-notch pilot, and lands the helicopter easily, despite the uneven surface. "Shut her down, Diego. I'm not sure long how long we'll be here. Might as well conserve the fuel."

"Roger that." The engine winds down, and very soon the propellers lie still.

I grab the cooler we brought with us, the one filled with hot packs and bags of blood. I knew whatever happened to Drew, he'd suffer damage from the sun. I slide open the door and jump out, grateful for the thickly-soled hiking boots to keep my purchase on the rock.

As I walk toward the line of trees, the four canines come barreling out. The large hound is dwarfed by the immense size of the werewolves. Despite looking like a wolf and having all the physical attributes of one, real wolves don't weigh the same as a grown man.

I motion for them to wait where they are, so we don't waste any more time. Once I arrive, cooler in hand, I address the boys, "Is Drew nearby?"

They both yip, in what sounds like a positive response. "I know it will take you both too long to change, can you lead me to him?"

Two more yips sound in the air and they turnaround, returning to the woods the way they came.

After a few minutes of following them through the forest, they refuse to go any further, pointing their noses toward a large tree with deep shade underneath. Unsure of their hesitancy, I decide to ease forward on my own. Whatever has happened to Drew, I know I'll be the only one who can safely handle him.

And judging by the younger wolves' desire not to come any closer, I'm guessing it certainly was something big that happened between the three of them. As I bend down and scoot under the canopy, the tree's darkness envelopes me, the temperature dropping several degrees already.

A loud hiss greets me from the darkness. "Drew? It's me. You're going to be okay."

I set the cooler down, open it, and pull out a bag of blood. One sharp fingernail pierces the top, and the scent of rich, warm blood seeps into the air. Strangled, garbled gasps followed by another hiss reveals exactly where Drew's body lies. He's on his side, his arms bound behind his back, and his bloodied face carries numerous open sores oozing fresh blood.

I've seen this type of reaction before, the fatal damage a vampire can receive from the sun. After a while, our natural healing ability is taxed so much it can no longer heal, and we become more susceptible and more damaged with every repeat exposure to the sun.

If anyone should know how sun exposure can eventually kill any vampire, it's me. It was my preferred method used on several ancients, one of whom was a deranged pedophile who really needed to die.

I have no experience saving someone from a situation like this. But, one thing I do know: blood cures all—at least for a vampire. I brush the leaves off his bound form, searching for whatever they used to tie him up. Before I have a chance to cut his bindings, he snaps at me. His teeth clamping down viciously on the air.

Deciding the way he is right now is as good a time as any to feed him, I bring the opening in the bag to his mouth and pour the blood in. He begins to gulp and choke, his hunger so intense, he's messy in his need and blood dribbles down the sides of his mouth, coating his face, mingling with the blood already on his skin.

The first pint is drained sooner than I would've expected. So I grab another and repeat the process. I brought four pints. And judging by his wounds, I still don't think it's going to be enough. "We'll get you to the inn and Dr. Cook's clinic as fast as possible. If you need to, you can feed from me on the ride back."

I'm wondering if he has a bit of sun poisoning along with the damage. Sun poisoning on a human is not quite the same as it is for a vampire. Enough sun poisoning can and will eventually drive the vampire mad.

My only hope is that we've reached him in time. His black eyes have me worried. After the first pint, they should have faded back to his normal brown color.

I'm glad I told Diego to turn off the helicopter, because by the time we're done at least forty minutes have gone by. The others have not come closer, and looking at Drew, I'm glad they didn't.

His wounds are healing, slowly, but he still hasn't spoken beyond a hiss or growl. Before giving him the last bag, I gently probe his mind. His mental pain and confusion is still high, telling me he needs more blood. Despite what I said to him earlier, it's too dangerous to share my blood with him while he's like this. With his eyes still black, he could easily snap and go after one of us on the helicopter—which is not something I'm willing to risk.

I'm going to need to knock him out. When Drew approaches the end of the pint, I cradle his head in both my hands and slip into his memories. Invading his mind is something I promised myself, and every member of my seethe, I would never do. But extenuating circumstances often call for extreme actions. Hopefully he can forgive me later when I tell him.

His mind is not what I expect—it's a hazy craze of bloodlust. This isn't good. I sift through the scattered surface emotions to delve deeper, but I resist acknowledging the damage I see. I'd like him to have more treatment—meaning blood and a long healing sleep—before I have to make a judgment call.

My shoulders slump, it's not a call I want to make for Drew. Or for anyone in my care, for that matter. Pushing away the subtle feelings of failure as they try to encase my spirit, I force him into a deep restorative sleep, the state his body would normally be in broad daylight. Hyped up on blood, he could easily stay awake, but with the deranged brain patterns I saw, it's definitely not safe.

When he's out, I lay him back and collect the empty bags, setting everything in the cooler. I walk out from the shade and deliver the cooler at Jon's feet. He, Pat, and Eric have all shifted back while I was with Drew, and judging by the clothes Jon is wearing, he must have returned to the helicopter to fetch his.

"How is he?" Jon asks.

I glance back at the shade under the tree. "I'm not sure."

"What do you mean you're not sure? From what they told me, he survived the crash."

"He made it." My eyes dart to Pat and Eric, then look away. "But he's not himself. Did he hurt you two?"

"Yes, ma'am. He did. We had to tie him up."

Jon looks shocked. "You tied up an injured vampire?"

Pat chimes in, his anxiety radiating off him. "We had no choice. We gave blood and helped him as long as we could. That's how we got as far as we did." He twists his hands, self-guilt evident in his tone. "But then something happened... He wasn't himself at the end. He went after us. We had to do something."

Eric nods, opening his mouth to add more.

I hold up my hands to stop him. "Relax. No one's mad at you. You did the right thing. He wouldn't have stopped until he killed you both."

Jon looks past me toward the tree. "What do you want to do?"

"I'm going to carry him back to the helicopter. I don't need any help, and I want you guys to stay clear until I have him secured inside. It's not that I don't trust the compulsion I put on him to sleep. It's..." I run my hands through my hair and sigh. "I'm not so sure how much of him is still there."

Eric looks distraught. Hands on his hips, he stares off at the tree, a tortured expression on his face. "What more could we have done? Is it our fault? Should we have buried him sooner and made him stay in the shade?"

"You did everything you could. Don't second-guess yourself. You guys traveled over thirty miles with him, were you aware you'd gone so far?"

Pat shakes his head, his self-disgust evident. He walks away, in the direction of the helicopter.

I look around the clearing. "Where's Candy? I was hoping I'd get to meet her."

"I asked her to stay back at the helicopter. She didn't bring any clothes with her and I wasn't sure what we'd be facing here. She's wearing an old jumpsuit and shoes left in the cabin from earlier. I told her to drink water and rehydrate after her long flight."

"Good. I'll meet you guys at the helicopter."

"Are you sure you don't need any help?" Eric asks. "I don't feel comfortable walking away and leaving him here for you. He's our friend. I feel like we let him down."

Jon pats him on the shoulder. "Trust me. She can handle it. Let's do as she's asked."

The three of them return to the helicopter and I go back and grab Drew. It takes a little maneuvering so I don't hurt him, but soon enough I've got him in a fireman's carry across both my shoulders. I move slowly hoping to not jostle him and cause any more injuries, but well aware his exposed skin can still be damaged by the sun during this transfer to the helicopter.

Within minutes, I arrive and quickly get his body wrapped in an emergency blanket and secured with tie-down straps. Once I nod to the others to load up, I give Diego the order to fire up the bird. Eric and Pat buckle in, sheer exhaustion adding years to their age, their faces hard-worn, dirty, and tired.

Soon, the others pile in and we're ready for liftoff. By mutual consent, we leave the door partly open for now, unwilling to trap ourselves in the tight confines of the cabin with the blood scent all over Drew. I settle back in my seat, closing my eyes for a moment. It'll take us at least two hours to get back to the resort. Grateful to have found all of them alive and intact, I refuse to think about the worst for Drew and focus on the positive. We're here, we're alive, and for now that's all that matters.

The wind whooshes past my ears, a welcome white noise to the worries swirling around in my brain. I open my eyes and look across the cabin toward Jon. He looks tired and mentally spent, the poor guy. He's put so much un-needed pressure on himself lately.

Candy and he sit close to each other, side-by-side and holding hands. She's a lovely looking young woman, long brown hair with a slight reddish cast to the color. She's fair-skinned with warm brown eyes in a heart-shaped face and a slender figure.

After a moment, Candy looks my way and stares fixedly at me, her face devoid of emotion and expression.

Jon glances at her sideways, then looks over at me, his eyebrows going up. "Vivian, meet Candy."

I smile, excited to meet the woman who makes Jon happy. Sure, I'll probably have to make her swear loyalty to me by the end of the day and exchange blood with her, but I'm still happy she's with him nonetheless. Not having buckled in yet, I shift my weight forward and offer her my hand, eager to make her acquaintance.

Without warning, she drops Jon's hand and leaps across the distance between us, something shiny and thin in her hands. Two fists go around my head and pull together revealing what she held is a silver chain, which cuts into my flesh, searing and burning. Before I have a chance to react, her skin touches mine and instantly I leap into her mind—

Images from the young woman's past flash by, in an

incoherent jumble. The first face I recognize is that of Persephone, smiling, tossing her head back and laughing, as she holds Candy's hand. Flashes of murderous intent flood the forefront of the shifter's mind, clouded over with Candy's thoughts: confusion, conflicted feelings, all overlain by intense mental pain. But the pain is not hers, it originates from Persephone, who's using it to control and manipulate her through multi-layered compulsions placed long ago.

All of this happens in the blink of an eye as Candy tightens the silver chain against my flesh. Jon's face transforms from smiling to horror as he screams "No!" from across the cabin and lunges forward to my defense.

Tossing her head back and forth, she looks like she's trying to fight the compulsion placed on her. The silver has cut through my flesh in the back and I feel it connecting with my spine, but still—I hesitate. I don't want to kill her if I can avoid it.

Candy stares into my eyes, her mind a wash of hatred. "You must die!"

Jon stretches his arms out, possibly to grab his crazed lover, but in his agitation and distress he brings on the half-shift. His hands elongate, claws sprouting from the tips. He reaches for her, unaware of his physical change, and his claws plunge through her back, piercing her lungs and heart. He screams again, this time shock filling his voice, "No!"

I reach up, grasping both sides of the thin, silver chain, forcing it apart. Candy sputters, slumping forward as blood bubbles from her mouth. Jon's horrified face appears over her shoulder, terror and fright billowing off him in waves. "Help me!" His panic snaps his control and he unwillingly completes his half-shift, his hands plunging deeper into his lover until the tips of his fingers emerge through her chest.

Eric unbuckles his seatbelt and lunges forward to clasp strong arms around Jon's middle, pulling him back from Candy. As he does so, the claws disappear into her chest and slide out her back, the smell of fresh blood filling the air as her lover's hands come away soaked in gore. Candy's eyes seek mine, the glow of hatred failing as the spark of her life snuffs out.

"Holy fucking hell!" Pat yells, scrambling to give Eric the support he needs in restraining their much stronger alpha in his larger wolfman form.

Removing Jon shifted Candy, throwing her, without meaning to, into the half-opened helicopter door. Her weight, and the sudden movement from all of us in the cabin, shift the helicopter, tilting it, causing Diego to yell from the front, "What the hell is going on back there?!"

Candy's body hits the door, sliding it open, and falls out of the helicopter into the ravine below.

Jon screams no over and over again. Pat and Eric physically hold him from leaping out of the helicopter after her. I unwind the chain from my neck and toss the offending blood-soaked silver across the cabin. My hands fly back to my wounds. The flow of blood has stopped, but not before running down my neck to soak my shirt. It all happened so fast I'm not sure what to do or say.

Pat slides the door shut, and returns to sitting on Jon's legs as Eric sits on his chest. In a moment, the alpha's horrified screams die down while the wound in my neck seals.

"Why? Why did she try and kill you?" He looks at me with tears streaming down his cheeks. "I don't understand. What happened?" He's blubbering and crying, snot and tears mixing on his confused face. "Oh my god, we have to go back. I hurt her bad."

Diego yells from the front, "Can someone tell me what's going on? Is everyone okay?"

"We're fine, man," Pat answers. "Just keep flying."

Jon thrashes on the floor. "No, no, no... we have to go back."

"Jon, I'm so sorry," I say in a whisper, easing to sit up in my seat. "She was dead before she fell."

I slip out of my chair and crawl across the floor to Jon. I cradle his crazed face in my hands and kiss his forehead, slipping into his mind to soothe his raging beast. "I'm sorry, Jon. She was a plant. She was the vampire servant of Persephone. She must've sent her to Romeo's pack months ago. Before we planned the big game hunt. That's the only thing I can think of."

He's calmer now, my presence helping him to shift back to his human form. Eric and Pat stay close to him, unwilling to leave their alpha when he's in so much obvious pain. "So I was a pawn, the whole time? I don't believe it. What she felt for me was real. We have to go back! What if she needs us? She could still be alive."

"Diego!" I shout, remembering I never had a chance to put my headset on. "Circle back. We need to see if we can find her."

The helicopter banks hard tossing us like ceramic dolls. Reminding us once again why you're supposed to buckle up. "Let me out!" Jon screams again. Pat and Eric pile back on when he moves for the sliding door. "Dammit, get off me!"

Reluctantly, Eric and Pat remove themselves from pinning

their alpha to the floor. Jon pops up and scrambles to the window searching for her body in the ravine below.

Diego circles the area we indicate once, then twice, and when we spot her lifeless body, he makes a note of the coordinates. She's down a cliff face and we don't have the equipment to recover her at this time. With sorrow, I make the hard choice to leave her body and tell Diego to continue home.

Jon cries anew when we turn north.

My heart aches for him. The betrayal so deep it hurts to breathe.

"She could still be suffering. We have to help her."

"Jon, you hit her heart. I know you didn't mean to, but I saw the light of life leave her eyes as you pulled your hands free. We can come back for her body later, we need to get Drew back to the inn safely."

Jon turns on me, rage distorting his features. "You. You did this. You didn't want me with her. Everything you said before was a lie."

Shock hits me like a slap in the face. There's only one way for him to understand. Without asking, I project Candy's memories to him, the ones I saw while she was choking me.

His face crumples as a sob escapes. "Can't be. It can't be."

He huddles on the floor and I go to him, wrapping my arms around him, holding on tighter when he attempts to shake me off. I will not leave him in his time of need.

Eric and Pat return to their seats, buckle up, and put on their headsets. They both nod at something the pilot must've said to them, and then make motions for Jon and me to buckle up as well. I refuse, telling them we're fine where we are, and continue to hold him.

Unwilling to look at me, Jon's eyes remain unfocused,

staring out the window, his body hunched in on itself, his shoulders slumping forward.

What can I possibly say to ease his pain? He meant to help me, and in his agitation, he skewered Candy through the back. This horrible tragedy is going to haunt him for a very long time.

We travel the rest of the way in silence, the return trip seeming much longer than our trip out. When we arrive, Jon is in a near catatonic state. Not speaking, refusing to move, and not looking at any of us.

The moment the helicopter reaches our property, I telepathically connect with Rafe and share everything that happened. He's there the second the door opens and lifts Jon into his arms. He transports him to a nearby SUV and climbs into the back with him, unwilling to leave him alone for a moment.

I fill in Diego with the barest of what happened, assuring him nothing was his fault. As we speak, Eric and Pat carry Drew's body on a makeshift gurney to another waiting vehicle. They're taking him to Dr. Cook's infirmary on the first floor of the apartment buildings.

As I walk toward the vehicle with Jon, feeling beat up and sick, the back door flies open. Jon bolts out in his wolf form, stumbling at first until he picks up speed and heads in the direction of his cabin.

His heartache and grief hit me like a physical pain, making me wish I could take it all away.

Rafe climbs out after him, shaking his head. "Will you go after him, or shall I?"

"I will. What he needs now is time. And a little space."

"Do you think he'd hurt himself? I don't want to leave him

alone for too long."

"I'm keeping mental tabs on him, the link is wide open between us whether he likes it or not. I can feel his grief and rage at himself—it's all-consuming at the moment. But you're right, I won't leave him alone for long." I reach up and wrap my arms around my husband. "He needs us both."

"Agreed." He tightens his hold on me, the grief spilling from Jon to us both.

"It was truly horrible."

"No one should ever have to discover a betrayal in such a way."

"And he wouldn't have if an ancient hadn't set their sights on killing me."

"Don't start blaming yourself, Dria. Persephone did this. Not you."

I sigh and pull from his embrace. "I know. But that doesn't make the pain any easier to bear."

Together, we make our way to the infirmary. I need to make sure Drew's going to be okay. One death is more than our family can handle today.

He's still as a corpse and pale as a ghost when we walk in.

Rafe grips my hand. "How's he doing, Dr. Cook?"

She looks up from the tubing leading to Drew's arm. "Good." She sees the look of dismay on my face and glances back at her patient's prone form. "Don't let his appearance fool you. He's not at death's door. He's still asleep, but I've been able to get three more pints in him the old fashioned way —by IV."

A breath I didn't know I was holding eases out, and the fist I've felt around my heart softens a little.

I nod, strengthening my resolve. I need to do it now,

whether I like it or not, before he wakes up. "Would you give us a moment with him?"

"Not a problem." She checks the level in his bag and nods to herself. "I'll be next door if you need me."

She closes the door on her way out, leaving Rafe and I alone with Drew's slumbering form.

"Dria, are you up for this? We could always bind him in silver and wait."

The thought of strapping silver around his chest and limbs leaves me shuddering. The memories of my own torture too close.

"No. I won't do that to him. It's best to check now and do what needs to be done."

I ease forward, dropping Rafe's hand. While I treasure the support he lends me, theres no way I want him exposed to the chaos swirling around in a sun-poisoned vampire brain.

Cautiously, I pick up Drew's limp hand. He's warmer than normal, more than likely due to the infusion of blood. Without further ado, I push my awareness through our physical connection, bracing myself for the horrors I saw earlier.

Instead of blood lust and an animal-like need to hunt and kill, I see healthy brainwaves and patterns. No thoughts of death and destruction, or gutting his lover anymore... simply peace.

My breath hitches and a sob escapes.

Rafe steps close behind, careful not to touch me. "What is it? Is he better or worse?"

A tear trickles down my cheek as I let go of Drew's hand and turn to face my husband. "He's going to be okay. We got him help in time."

Rafe reaches up and catches a tear on his thumb. "I'm glad

to hear it." His palm caresses my skin, leaving warmth in its wake. "Jon isn't the only one on shaky emotional ground." He pulls me into his arms, his strong chest pressing firmly to mine.

The flood gates open and I cry, the first time I can remember doing so in decades. Long and deep, my shoulders hunching under the flood of emotions. As my breath hitches and my nose runs, Rafe holds me throughout, whispering soothing words and trailing a hand up and down my back in comfort.

After a while, the pain lessens and the tears slow. "I—I don't like caring about all these people," I say, my voice raw with feeling. "I want it to be just you and I again. It's easier with only the two of us."

Rafe hands me a tissue from a box on the counter and I blow my nose. "Easier isn't always better."

"I can't handle the loss."

He eases back and stares into my tear-filled eyes. "Yes, you can. Look at what loving them has brought you."

"Snot and tears? No thanks."

"Darling, listen to yourself. When was the last time you cared enough to cry? Loving them has helped return some of your humanity to you."

I stop, surprised by his comment. He's right. Dammit. I pull away and scrub a hand over my face. "Great, my husband has a fetish for cryers. Good to know."

He steps closer, into my personal space, making it impossible to brush him off with humor. "You will not ignore this. It's important. Face it. Own it. You care about our seethe. And in doing so, you've become a better person."

"Okay, fine." I grab more tissues and dry my face as best I can. "I'm a better person. Isn't that terrific." After tossing the tissues in the garbage, I turn to him. "What next? Do I write them all letters detailing how important they are in my life? Seriously, hon. I can't handle more."

"I'm sorry, but there's still one more person who needs us."

The burning in my eyes begins again, and I curse my return of "humanity" as Rafe put it.

"Jon," he says. "We must see to Jon."

We leave and I send a text to the doctor explaining Drew's mental situation. I didn't want her to see me like this. I'd rather no one saw me at my weakest.

Rafe's mental energy reaches out to mine. *Caring about others isn't a weakness.*

"Can we talk about it later?" I ask. "I can't handle more self-analyzation at the moment."

He nods and we travel the rest of the way in silence. Within minutes we're pulling in front of Jon's cabin. As we approach his front door, something feels off. Like he's not inside.

"Wait," I say while coming to a halt. I extend my consciousness and discover he's not in his home. I reach out, pushing myself further, determined to locate him wherever he is.

I find him, his mental signature slightly altered while in his wolf form. "He's with his dogs. In the kennel. They are all curled up in a big dog pile."

I turn back to the jeep and Rafe stops me. "Either you go in, or I will. But we're not leaving him alone."

"Yes. You're right. I just..."

"You *can* handle this, Dria. He needs you. Now more than ever."

"It will hurt."

"I know. You are strong enough to handle the pain. I'm here. You're not alone. More importantly, Jon needs to feel that, too."

It takes almost an hour of cajoling, and a little bit of begging on my part, before Jon will leave the kennel. When he does, we take him back to our place and stretch out on the big couch where we used to watch Rafe's movie marathons together.

He hasn't changed back from a wolf yet, and that's okay. Whatever he needs to deal with the pain is fine by me.

I wrap my arms around his big furry body, snuggling myself along his back. "I'm here for you, Jon. Please don't hate me for what's happened." Unbidden, the tears return to my eyes. "I love you."

Surprisingly, Rafe sits down near Jon's head. Easing the large wolf skull onto his lap, he wraps a hand deeply into the fur at Jon's neck. "I love you, too, you big furball."

Rafe's mental voice touches my mind. *Sleep, liebling. You need to rest.*

I stare at the dancing eternal flame set on the side table and wish I could hurl myself into its depths.

Quiet your mind. Only then will you find peace.

I wrap my delicate psyche in the warmth of his love and will myself to relax. We will overcome this. Together. There is no other choice.

The next day, Asa's tight voice projects through the call-button speaker on our living room phone.

"Vivian? Do you have a minute? I need you to see something."

My entire body tenses at his tone. Good God, I need a freakin' break. There's only so much a powerful vampire can take in one week. "I'll be down in a minute."

I struggle to my feet, knowing I'll have to repeat the mate-bond ritual again tonight whether I want to or not, and make my way downstairs to the command center. "What is it? You sounded serious."

"Come, take a look at this. I'm not sure what to make of it, besides the obvious."

I glance down at the screen to see...

Vivian,

This message is part of an early warning response system. If you're receiving it, I and all my employees have been out of contact with our computer system for over 24 hours. Please check and see if we're all okay.

This is not a test, nor is it a joke. If we're not able to get to a computer, or a phone, something is seriously wrong, and you're my back-up plan. If you don't reach me personally, fly here. We need you.

~Cy

A cold, tendril slips down my spine. Whatever has happened, it can't be good.

"Were you able to get a hold of him yesterday about the list?"

"No, I wasn't. I left a voicemail and figured we'd hear from him or my Aunt Cali later today."

"Did you try your Aunt's cell?"

Asa nods, his expression grim. "What do you think it means?"

"I think it means he's in danger and we better get the hell out there as quick as we can." My mind starts to whirl with all the small tasks that need to be completed before we can get in the air.

The worst part is we aren't quite ready to get on the road to track down my turns, but it looks like we're getting underway whether we like it or not. "Call the pilots, wake them up. Call the hangar, tell them to prepare the jet." I check my watch. "We need to be in the air as fast as possible. Worst case scenario, if something happened to him on his property, we won't have a lot of time before the local authorities get on the scene, if they're not there already."

"Yes, ma'am," Asa says, reaching for the phone. "Who else is going?" There's a hint of eagerness in his voice.

"Let me talk to Rafe and I'll let you know."

His face falls, correctly guessing what the answer will turn out to be. Hey, I did warn them that no one would be flying with the three of us to find my turns.

Rafe? I ask telepathically, through our mental connection. *Wake up, love. We've got trouble with a capital T, and we need to start packing.*

I take the basement steps two at a time, using vampire speed to get to the top as fast as I can. I zip through our kitchen, down the hall, and into our bedroom, right as Rafe is stretching in bed.

"What's up, liebling?" He glances at the clock. "It's not like you to wake me after only an hour of sleep." His expression changes to concern, "Is it Jon, is he okay?"

I touch Jon's erratic mind. "He's okay for now. Not sure after I tell him what's happened."

"Okay, out with it. What's going on?"

"Cy has an emergency notification system set up via his computer system. It's basically an automated SOS."

"Really? Did you know he'd done that?"

"Nope, not at all. But here's the issue—it went off. He's in trouble, and by the sounds of it, so is his entire seethe."

"Shit. What do we do? We've got our plates pretty damn full as it is. Asa hasn't finished scanning all the journals yet. And last I checked, we only have one facial recognition match from the sketches so far."

"We don't have a choice, Rafe. He's on the list. His distress call may very well be related to Rolando and Persephone. And after what just happened with Candy, I'd say it probably does relate to them."

He runs a hand over his tired-looking face. "Crap. I guess we don't have a choice then. Should I start packing?"

"Yes. We need to leave immediately." I stand and head for the closet. "Who do you want to come with us?"

"Jon, obviously. There's no way I'd leave him here alone in his current state." Pain laces his tone.

"Agreed. He shouldn't be alone, and we need him. No matter what, he's our most trusted friend. I can't imagine going anywhere without him guarding our backs."

"That's settled," Rafe says. "Let's pack, keeping in mind we've got one grieving werewolf joining us and a group of manipulator vampires gunning for us."

"And how do you pack for that?"

"Weapons. You pack a lot of weapons."

~~*~~

A personal note from C.J.: If you enjoyed this book, please consider leaving a review on the product page where you purchased it. Reviews help readers discover new series and perhaps try an author they never heard of.

~Thank you!

To receive notice of my next release, please join my newsletter! Copy and paste this link into your browser window: smarturl.it/cjenews

Other Titles by C.J. Ellisson

The *V V Inn* Series:
Death's Servant (prequel story)
Vampire Vacation
The Hunt
Big Game
Death Times Two
Blood Legacy
Sharpen the Blade
Blood Reckoning (coming soon!)

Romance Titles:
Vanilla on Top
Vanilla Spice
Avoiding Mr. Right
Loving Ms. Wrong
Johnny Living Dangerously (erotica)

ABOUT THE AUTHOR

C.J. Ellisson is a *New York Times* & *USA Today* bestselling author, who writes supernatural suspense, mystery, and romance. She lives in northern Virginia with her husband, two teenagers, three dogs, and two cats—reporting to love the energetic zoo that's become their home.

When forced to give up a career due to her decreasing health, C.J. turned to writing in 2009 and claims the escape helped save her sanity. She battled severe chronic illness for years and has finally reached the end of her long-term treatment.

Instead of dozens of pills, IVs, exhaustion, and pain, C.J.'s life is now filled with writing, exercising, eating healthy, and running a novel-writing club at her daughter's school. It all leads to a fun-filled, busy day, and she's incredibly grateful to be so involved in life again.

C.J. loves to hear from readers! Connect with her at:
www.cjellisson.com
cj@cjellisson.com

ACKNOWLEDGMENTS

Unlike other books, I do not have a laundry list of people I'd like to thank on this one. Plain and simple, I'm thanking YOU, my readers.

I almost quit. I gave up several times. I wanted to walk away from writing.

My readers kept me going. And for that, I will be forever grateful. Thank you.

GLOSSARY

Asa ~ the fledgling vampire sent by Cy, who was turned in Afghanistan while serving in the Army.

Blood Bond ~ a term used to describe the exchange of blood between either a human and a vampire, both ways, or a master vampire and a member of their seethe. It enables telepathic communication between them through the bond, if desired.

Blood Coffee ~ a mixture of half-blood and half-coffee, favored by undead everywhere.

Blood Donor ~ a person who willingly donates blood via a bag, or direct from their body, to a vampire for sustenance.

Bonded Mate ~ a deeper connection than a servant, this bond allows the non-vampire to stop aging and share a significant amount of power associated with the bonded vampire. A complex ritual and exchange of large amounts of blood must take place for this bond to occur. The only way to break the bond is through death or a rare, deep mind manipulation severing the link.

Bunny ~ Paul's wife.

Candy ~ A newer member of Romeo's pack, who lived with them disguised as a male werewolf named Spike.

Cali ~ Cy's bonded mate, and a werewolf. She's also Asa's aunt.

Companion ~ a human who has donated blood to a vampire and been accepted into the vampire's care for future feedings.

Cy ~ Vivian's contact in New York, whom she turned when she discovered him close to death in an alley outside his bar over forty-five years ago.

Diane ~ Dr. Cook's adult daughter and a witch.

Dr. Margery Cook ~ the onsite doctor on the property should a problem with a human arise.

Drew ~ one of the new member's of Vivian's seethe.

Dria ~ the master vampire who narrates the first book, aka Vivian and Alexandria.

Eric ~ a new werewolf from Romeo's pack.

Enforcer ~ a highly skilled vampire assassin, used as an instrument of justice by the Tribunal.

Fledgling ~ term used for a vampire under the age of five years.

Jonathan ~ Vivian's werewolf servant and the head groundskeeper on the property.

Liebling ~ German endearment, meaning darling.

Manipulator ~ a rare breed of vampire able to mind control other vampires. Usually hunted down and killed by their own kind to ensure they do not gain power over their fellow vampires.

Master Vampire ~ a vampire who heads his or her own seethe, or is independent of a seethe. One not requiring the blood of a master to gain in power, but has accumulated enough strength to hold their own in a battle where an older vampire may try to drain a younger one for his or her blood.

Mate ~ see **Bonded Mate.**

Michelle ~ aka Chelly, an employee at the inn, who also doubles as a blood donor,

Pat ~ a new werewolf, originally from Romeo's pack.

Old Blood ~ a term used to describe the blood a seethe member gets from a master to increase an individual's own power. Contains the added benefit of increasing a vampire's perceived undead age if the blood is strong enough and consumed regularly.

Paul ~ a gourmet chef imported from the lower forty-eight, married to Bunny and a newly-turned vampire who is also part of Vivian's seethe.

Rafe ~ Vivian's bonded mate for sixty-five years, and co-owner to the inn.

Rogue ~ term used to describe a vampire who has either gone a little bat-shit crazy or who has been deemed a criminal by the Tribunal.

Rolando ~ part of the Tribunal of Ancients, located in Argentina.

Romeo ~ Jonathan's old Alpha, but not the Were who changed him.

Seethe - A vampire family, or group of vampires, with a master vampire at its head.

Servant ~ see **Vampire Servant**

Tommy ~ an employee, originally from Australia, who mainly works the front desk and organizes the blood donor list for the guests.

Tribunal of Ancients ~ the governing body of ruling ancient vampires, entrusted with maintaining the secrecy of the existence of vampires from the human race.

Turning ~ term used for when a human has been changed into a vampire.

Vampire Servant ~ a human, or Were, who has donated to and ingested the blood of a vampire. A mind connection can be established (and broken), allowing telepathic communication. The servant feels a desire to protect and serve the vampire above his or her own needs.

Vivian ~ the nickname for Dria, a play on words from *The V V Inn*.

Were ~ shorthand for werewolf.